AF280974

Edition Liguria

Caponnetto Investigates – Book 2

The Book

Spring is just beginning in Liguria. Caponnetto's initial delight about his part in catching a murderer with *Commissario* Bonfatti is short-lived. Just as he is about to turn his attention back to the Osteria Il Golfo and its attractive tenant Giulia, his past starts to catch up with him.

A prison escape in Munich alerts both the Bavarian State Criminal Police as well as law enforcement in Italy. Between *zuppa* and *dolce*, Caponnetto is forced to admit that although his time as a *Carabiniere* is officially at an end, it is far from over.

The Author

Enrico Palumbo was born in 1972 in Karlsruhe, Germany, and studied in Munich and Venice. He started his career as a journalist for German and Italian news agencies and media before moving into business. After working in various places, such as Prague, Milan and Zurich, he returned to Karlsruhe, where he has been living since 2019. "Deadly Caffè" is his second novel in the murder mystery series about the retired *Carabiniere* Giuseppe Caponnetto.

ENRICO PALUMBO

DEADLY CAFFÈ

A Ligurian Murder Mystery

This novel's story and characters are fictitious. Certain long-standing institutions, agencies, and public offices are mentioned, but the characters involved are wholly imaginary.

Edition Liguria

This title is also available as an e-book.

The German National Library lists this publication in the Deutsche Nationalbibliografie; detailed bibliographic data can be accessed on the Internet at http://dnb.dnb.de.

Contact: Edition.Liguria[at]web.de
Editing: Edition Liguria

English translation: Suzanne Pfleger

Cover photo: monticello

Publisher: BoD · Books on Demand GmbH,
Überseering 33, 22297 Hamburg,
bod@bod.de
Print: Libri Plureos GmbH,
Friedensallee 273, 22763 Hamburg

ISBN: 978-3-7693-5185-9

Chi nasce tondo non può morire quadrato.

Those born round cannot die square.

Italian saying

I

Caponnetto was up early. He could hear the birds singing. The air smelled of spring.

If you don't live by the sea and only spend a few days there once in a while, you might not notice that the sea smells different in spring. It's fresh, invigorating, and less salty than in winter. Sometimes it even smells slightly earthy, with a sweet note reminiscent of flowers. This is due to the algae, which multiply as temperatures begin to rise, and to the spring breezes, which transport their different fragrances from the sea to the coast.

Spring is Caponnetto's time. It's the season when he has always felt particularly inspired, full of energy and drive.

Three weeks ago, he had got on his new sports bike early in the morning for the first time. Since then, he had been leaving his apartment at the port of Savona every day at around 8 am. This morning routine was good for him.

But today, he started his tour earlier than usual. That was the only reason the men in the black SUV missed him. They would wait for him – that was their job.

After his accident on the Via Aurelia eight months ago, Caponnetto had gone through various phases. At first, in hospital, he was in denial about how his injuries would affect his service with the *Carabinieri*. Then, with his artificial knee, came the certainty that things would never be the same again. And with this realisation came anger: 'Why me? Why now?'

Back then, he was convinced that he'd simply been in the wrong place at the wrong time. He wanted to believe that the collision on the coastal road between Finale Ligure and Noli had been a tragic hit-and-run accident.

During the rehabilitation phase, Caponnetto thought about how he could continue his work investigating the *Agromafia* despite his limited fitness for duty. He came to the conclusion that he didn't want to do things by halves and decided to quit altogether. Then, when his *Zia* Antonella died unexpectedly, his grief for his aunt eclipsed his grief for his old life.

On the very day of his retirement, Caponnetto had become involved in a new case with his friend *Commissario* Bonfatti. Together they had solved the murder of an old man. They hadn't expected to be showered with praise, but neither had they expected to be mired in controversy.

Caponnetto didn't want to find himself in such a situation again. Especially not now in spring. He had ideas, he had plans. His life was almost perfect – if it hadn't been for the matter with Stefania. But there was always something!

*

Commissario Bonfatti was sitting behind his desk on the third floor of the *Questura* in Savona, leafing through the local section of La Stampa in a leisurely fashion. There was currently no case of public interest in his jurisdiction. So today he hoped that his own face wouldn't be jumping out at him from the newspaper again. He usually found the photos of himself rather unflattering – not to mention the text accompanying them.

For several days after the 'Serra case', the local papers had gleefully exploited the story: The front page article 'Ex-*Carabiniere* saves failed police investigation' was followed by one with the headline 'Police solve murder case – thanks to the *Carabinieri*!' Finally, on the third day, they printed the question, 'Who's better: the police or the *Carabinieri*?' There were no facts in the article and the only quotes were from a street survey.

As if there wasn't already enough controversy about the cooperation between the *Polizia di Stato* and the *Carabinieri*!

Today, the local section was dominated by a report on the archaeological excavations in Albisola. The provincial administration had raised money from an EU fund to resume work at a country villa dating back to Roman times.

The villa was one of the archaeological remains from the Alba Docilia period. This ancient city stood on the site of the current municipality of Albisola Superiore and was located at an important junction of the roads connecting Rome with the Ligurian coast and later with southern Gaul. This strategic location made Alba Docilia an important centre for trade and transport. It was also during this time that the tradition of ceramics and pottery in the region had its origins. To this day, Albisola is an important centre for ceramics in Italy.

The city council and local businesses in Albisola hoped that the excavations would generate additional tourism from the other provinces of Liguria and Piedmont. Advertisements had been running for weeks, and both local and national media were reporting on the preparations for the excavations.

Somehow they even managed to lure a television team from RAI, Italy's state broadcasting company, to the small coastal town, who had even reported about it on their third program, before the ground-breaking ceremony, which was to be held today.

Malicious gossips claimed that the niece of one of the Albisola city council members had a friend whose brother-in-law played paddle in Rome with a man whose brother was a porter at RAI who knew an editor who worked for TG3, the regional news channel on the third Italian television channel. The editor then announced in a conference with the regional studios that he'd like to broadcast more in-depth reports on Italy's ancient roots. This was how they managed to get the topic on the agenda of the TG3 regional editorial office in Genoa.

'They should go ahead and report more about cultural matters instead of focussing on murder and manslaughter,' thought Bonfatti. His mobile phone rang. The *Commissario* looked at the display and answered the call.

"*Buon giorno, Dottore* Hering," Bonfatti was glad that the *Kriminalhauptkommissar* or Detective Chief Superintendent of the Bavarian State Criminal Police spoke Italian so well, because his German was non-existent and his English was more than a little rusty.

"Hello, old chap. How's our friend?"

"May I be frank?"

"Yes, please."

"He's gone back into his shell."

"And that means?"

"He pushed me away, just like he did with you. I've tried to talk to him several times since you called me, but he's stubborn. Caponnetto says he's not interested in the matter, he wants to move on, blah blah blah ..."

"And what do you think?"

"I have no idea why he's behaving like this. But although my hands are tied, I have, of course, tried to do something within my limited power."

"I'm dying to know what it is," said Hering, leaning back in his chair and looking out of his Munich office window at the Marsstrasse.

"Well, as I said, unfortunately, my hands are tied. The reporting on our investigation into the murder case, ..." Bonfatti hesitated.

"Yes, I heard about it," said Hering dryly. "Caponnetto sent me a copy of the newspaper ..."

"The one with the photo where I look so stupid?" asked the *Commissario*.

Hering cleared his throat. "Yes, I believe there was a photo of you in the newspaper too."

"And it's now hanging on the wall in your office in Munich next to the one of your *Minister-President*?" asked Bonfatti, laughing.

"No, old chap, I passed the newspaper on. I understood the message that Caponnetto was sending me with it," replied Hering.

"You mean that he's getting more attention than he'd like and he wants to be left alone?" asked Bonfatti.

"Yes," retorted Hering. "Incidentally, I passed the newspaper on to Simone Noce."

Simone Noce, known as *U Muto*, 'The Mute', had been convicted several times in absentia and had been on the run for over ten years. But during cross-border investigations, *U Muto* had been unexpectedly caught by investigators from the Bavarian State Criminal Police Office a few weeks ago when an officer recognised him by his voice during a wiretapping operation. Noce had undergone thyroid surgery in his early 30s. The surgeon had inadvertently injured one of the muscles that control the larynx. Since then, Noce's voice had been impaired and he rarely spoke. Instead, he communicated with gestures or wrote small notes. When he did say something, his voice sounded like a whisper, sometimes like a croak.

The surgeon who had operated on Noce disappeared a few weeks after the surgery. A few days later, the doctor was found strangled in the trunk of his car – with his tongue cut out.

Noce's physical disability had not hindered his rise in the criminal organisation. On the contrary, *U Muto* had become the embodiment of a saying popular among Mafiosi: 'Those who know, do not speak; those who speak, do not know.'

"Two days ago I questioned Noce again when I brought him the newspaper," said Hering.

Bonfatti blinked. "And?" he asked, although he could guess the answer.

"Well, what do you think? He lived up to his nickname," replied Hering.

"*Chi sa, non parla; chi parla, non sa*," said the *Commissario*, quoting the saying in question.

"Yes, exactly," confirmed Hering, and told Bonfatti how, at the end of the interrogation, he had played Noce the phone call in which the assassination attempt on Caponnetto was mentioned: 'The *Capitano* has received our message. He won't cause us any more trouble, and if he does, we know where to find him.'

The words could be heard loud and clear. It wasn't Noce who had spoken, but a man whose identity the police didn't yet know. Hering had asked Noce about the identity of the man who had allegedly ordered the assassination of Caponnetto. But *U Muto* had only raised his chin slightly and clicked his tongue gently against the roof of his mouth, which produced a sharp, dismissive tone.

"Very well, *Signor* Noce. I understand," Hering had replied, taking the copy of La Stampa out of his pocket.

"You can keep the newspaper anyway. Consider it a greeting from your homeland because you won't be seeing it again anytime soon."

That had been two days ago. Now, just as Hering and Bonfatti were talking about him, Simone Noce was planning his escape. *U Muto* wanted – no, *had* to – get to Italy and take care of a very urgent matter.

*

The younger of the two men in the black SUV drummed his fingers impatiently on the steering wheel.

"We should call and say what's going on."

"Relax," replied the man in the passenger seat, "he's probably just late today. You'll see, he'll be out soon."

"And if not?"

"Then we can always call in ten minutes."

He had barely finished the sentence when his mobile rang. The two men looked at each other, casting their eyes around the inside of the SUV as if they expected to see a microphone.

"Don't tell me you've lost him?!" barked the man through the hands-free system. The two of them sat up in their seats. They cast their eyes around again. They stayed silent, embarrassed.

"No answer is also an answer. I thought so! Drive to Pietra Ligure immediately. If he doesn't show up there by midday today, go back to Savona. And call me as soon as you have visual contact again. Understood?"

The man hung up without waiting for an answer.

"Drive," said the passenger, "and keep your mouth shut!"

The driver pressed the start button and drove the SUV towards the Autostrada dei Fiori.

Most days Caponnetto would head east from Savona in the morning. He would cycle towards the rising sun, up over the ridge, past the hospital, *Ospedale* San Paolo, and back to the coastal road towards Albisola. Piazza Matteotti was his turning point.

At the Pilar Bar, he would drink a cappuccino, eat a brioche and leaf through the newspapers. He would then take the shorter route back to Savona along the Via Aurelia.

In the days when he was still on active duty, he would never have allowed himself such routines – routines make people predictable. And people who are predictable make easy targets.

Today he had got up earlier because he was planning a longer trip in the opposite direction. His destination was Pietra Ligure. He wanted to check on the house he inherited from his aunt, where he sometimes stayed the night, and which was partly still being renovated.

For lunch, he was planning to go to the Osteria Il Golfo, which was also part of his late aunt's estate. The thought of seeing the tenant of the *osteria* made him a little uneasy. But avoiding Giulia wasn't a long-term solution.

He was dreading meeting the attractive woman again, as it reminded him of what a fool he'd been. Just when he and Giulia were about to become closer, he had allowed Stefania to hijack him.

His ex-girlfriend had more or less unexpectedly turned up on his doorstep. If only he'd listened to his gut feeling that evening and prepared the guest bed for Stefania! But things had turned out differently, and since then he had been feeling guilty towards Giulia, although this was completely unnecessary. Nothing whatsoever had happened between him and Giulia. They had seen each other several times at the *osteria*, which bound them together as tenant and landlord. With each encounter, Giulia had been a little friendlier towards him. He had made an effort to get to know her better and was open about his interest in her. But then Stefania had come to visit from Milan and everything was turned upside down. He had believed that the night could have heralded a new beginning with her. However, Stefania surprised him that morning, before breakfast, with the news that she would be moving to the European Public Prosecutor's Office in Luxembourg.

Caponnetto remembered that Stefania had often spoken about the EPPO, which investigates serious cross-border financial crimes, particularly VAT and subsidy fraud against the EU. However, the fact that Stefania now wanted to move to Luxembourg had surprised him and was also a clear signal to Caponnetto that she didn't want to commit herself – at least not to him.

To make matters worse, they had an argument before they parted. Once again, it was due to a misunderstanding between them. Caponnetto had pulled a face when Stefania told him that she was moving to Luxembourg – partly out of dis-appointment, but also because he was somewhat frustrated with himself.

Stefania had interpreted his reaction differently. She thought he disapproved of her involvement with the EPPO because she was the one who would now be dealing with the *Agromafia* and she would outshine him with her successes.

Contrary to popular belief, the adulteration of olive oil and other forms of label fraud are just one area of the *Agromafia's* crimes. Much greater profits are made by subsidy-fraud and food-smuggling. Stefania would certainly be dealing with the *Agromafia* at the EPPO, but nothing was further from Caponnetto's mind than such rivalries and comparisons. Especially since he had officially retired. The fact that Stefania still hadn't realised this, still didn't understand him, annoyed Caponnetto more than her accusation that he didn't wish her success. So they parted ways before Caponnetto could tell her about the text message he had received the previous evening.

'Need to talk. It's about your accident,' was what the message said.

Caponnetto hadn't reacted at first. Later, after the argument and Stefania had left, he had felt empty and lonely.

It was in this state of mind that Caponnetto had picked up his mobile phone that morning and tapped out a reply to *Kriminalhauptkommissar* Manfred Hering's text message, which sounded much more dismissive than intended.

The woman with red hair rolled up the mat and tightened the elastic band. She looked at her smartwatch and wondered how much time she had left. 'I'll wash my hair tomorrow,' she thought, taking off her top on the way to the bathroom.

In front of the mirror, she looked at her abs with satisfaction and then gently stroked the slightly hardened area below her collarbone with her left index finger. She put her thumb on it and moved it in a circular motion from the inside to the outside with light pressure. Finally, she turned to the side and looked first at her biceps, then at her shoulder blade. The scar where the bullet had entered appeared far less severe than the one on her back where it had exited. The wound there had been larger and the scar was more difficult to care for.

Her bullet-proof vest had stopped two bullets: one at the level of her navel and one slightly above the base of her breastbone. The third bullet had hit her on the outer edge of the vest next to the Velcro fastener – luckily it was a clean shot right through.

She took off her leggings and underpants and got into the shower. They were expecting her in one hour. Then she would get a new assignment – finally!

*

"*Avanti*", called *Commissario* Bonfatti, and Francesca Nobile entered his office.

"*Buon giorno, Ispettore*! How was the training course in Bologna?"

"*Buon di, Commissario*! It was very interesting. We spent a whole day talking about mozzarella – how the *Agromafia* uses illegal growth hormones to increase the milk production of buffalos, mixes their milk with normal cow's milk or milk powder to cut costs, and speeds up the coagulation process with lime."

"That sounds pretty disgusting," remarked her colleague Gianni Sestri, who had stepped in behind her and pulled a face.

"Don't tell me that Nobile spoiled your appetite, Sestri!" teased Bonfatti. Nobile stepped aside so that Bonfatti and Sestri could look at each other directly.

"Uh, no, *Signor Commissario*. But since you're asking, I'd like to take a break now."

"Is that why you've come to see me?" asked Bonfatti, who had noticed that Sestri was holding a piece of paper in his hand. He pointed twice with the index finger of his right hand in the direction of Sestri's left, then turned his wrist and, with his index finger, beckoned Sestri to come over. Sestri looked first at Nobile, then back at the *Commissario* and took two steps forward.

"I'd really like to take a short break and get something to eat ..."

"The piece of paper, Sestri. What does it say?" asked Bonfatti impatiently.

"A body was found during the excavations in Albisola," Sestri stammered, "but it's a very old one. So there's no rush!"

"How old?" asked Nobile.

"Well, between 20 and 25 years old."

"But what are you talking about, *Agente*? 25 years isn't old," exclaimed Bonfatti indignantly.

"I think he means the body has been dead for 20 years or more, right?" interjected Nobile.

Sestri nodded vigorously.

"That's right. The people at the site said the body must have been there for over 20 years."

"Ah, and that's why you think we could have a *caffè* and eat a *focaccia* before we leave?" asked Bonfatti.

"Yes, exactly," said Sestri, relieved.

The young policeman's face beamed until he noticed Nobile's piercing gaze. His colleague shook her head almost imperceptibly.

"Well, I'll go and get the car, *Signor Commissario*," said Sestri sheepishly.

Bonfatti turned to Nobile: "And you're coming with me!"

*

In Pietra Ligure, the black SUV drove along Viale Europa towards Via S. Francesco. The two men knew they couldn't park directly in front of Caponnetto's house. They would be noticed immediately. So they looked for a side street or a building that would provide good cover while allowing them to see Caponnetto should he approach his house.

"Well, I'm telling you, we're just wasting our time here," grumbled the older of the two men.

"Why should Caponnetto cycle to Pietra Ligure today of all days when he usually heads off in the other direction?"

The man at the wheel looked at his fingernails and shook his head.

"Pasquale, you think too much. And you talk too much. We've been told to wait in Pietra, so we'll wait in Pietra. *Basta!*"

"Still, I'd like to know why the old man is so sure that we should wait here today and not somewhere else."

"He has his sources. We don't need to know any more. I don't, and you don't either. *Hai capito*?"

"Yes, of course I understand," growled Pasquale, "don't ask questions, just follow orders."

*

Caponnetto had first noticed the SUV a few days ago in Savona. The model itself wasn't unusual; vehicles of this type were often seen on the streets, but the tinted windows had caught his attention. Then he thought he recognised the car in the car park of the old train station in Albisola and had memorised the license plate. Next time he, would check whether it was the same car, should there be a next time.

During all his years in the service of the *Carabinieri*, he had become accustomed to taking note of his surroundings, paying attention to any irregularities and deviations. And to anything that didn't fit in, such as a motorcyclist wearing a helmet in Palermo. What would be viewed as a normal safety measure elsewhere might spell danger on the streets of Palermo or Naples, if a killer was hiding behind the helmet. Hardly anyone ever wore a helmet there, so a rider who suddenly appeared wearing one might well be a threat.

Even a vehicle you see several times over the course of a few days might spell danger. With this in mind, it was a lucky coincidence for Caponnetto that a Fiat 500 cut him off at the intersection of Via Soccorso and Via S. Francesco.

To avoid a collision, Caponnetto turned right into Via Soccorso on his sports bike instead of continuing straight ahead. He planned to take two left turns and come back onto Via S. Francesco just above the playground.

However, just as he was turning into Via Alberti, he saw a black SUV at the end of the street. Caponnetto turned around immediately.

*

The metal fence that had been erected to keep overly curious visitors to the excavations at a distance now formed a natural barrier for securing the crime scene. This facilitated the work of the law enforcement officers who were the first to arrive on the scene after it had been reported by the archaeologists.

When they recognised Bonfatti, the men lifted the metal fence to one side to let the *Commissario* into the area behind the barrier.

A skeleton, mostly uncovered, lay under a white tent. Cristina Donati knelt next to it and was taking photos.

"*Signor Commissario,*" she said in greeting and winked at Bonfatti. He smiled back and replied: "And, *Signora* Pathologist, what have you got for me today?"

"Male, I can't say exactly how old he was at the time of death. Maybe in his late 20s, possibly early 30s. Otherwise, I agree with the archaeologists. The body has probably been here for 20 or 25 years. I'll be finished with the paperwork soon, then we can remove the body. You'll get the final report in the next few days, and the first results maybe by this evening."

"Oh, one more reason to look forward to this evening," Bonfatti replied.

Nobile rolled her eyes. Since her boss and the forensic pathologist had become a couple again, she had to endure this flirtatious behaviour quite often.

The *Commissario* looked at his young colleague.

"What do you think, *Ispettore*?"

"Well, he probably didn't just get into the hole and cover himself up, so someone must have put him there."

"But why here?"

"Well, this isn't a bad place to permanently hide a body: the excavations have been on hold for decades. If the body were buried somewhere in a field where houses are to be built after a few years…"

"When the construction workers start to dig, something that was supposed to remain in the dark forever suddenly comes to light …," interjected the *Commissario*, adding, "on the other hand, this hiding place isn't easy to access. You have to climb over the high fence…"

"Excuse me, *Commissario*, that's not quite true. The fence didn't used to be so high, so it was easy to get onto the site," interrupted Nobile.

"Oh? And how do you know that?"

"I grew up nearby and as a child I often went to the beach in Albisola with my family. For my sister and me, the excavation site was something like an adventure playground."

Bonfatti took his mobile phone out of his jacket pocket.

"It's already past noon," he exclaimed. "You can manage here on your own, surely, Nobile? I need to leave. I'll see you later at the *Questura*. You and Sestri will find a lift back, right?"

And without waiting for an answer, the *Commissario* hurried away, asking an astonished Sestri to get out of the car before he drove off.

In front of the door, the woman with red hair tucked a stray lock back behind her left ear. She was now wearing a tight silvery-grey knitted dress and cream-coloured trainers. Her knock was answered immediately.

"Just a moment, please." Then the door opened. "Slight change of plan, Wagner. Come with me," said the Head of Department 62. He walked diagonally across the corridor to another office. He knocked, opened the door without waiting for a response, and stuck his head in.

"She's here!" he said, pulling his head back out, stepping aside to let her in. *Kriminalhauptkommissar* Hering stood up and walked out from behind his desk.

"Hello, Ms. Wagner, pleased to meet you. I'm Manfred Hering."

Andrea Wagner shook his hand. "Something has come up that requires a change of plan. Please, do take a seat."

Wagner took two steps forward and, as she sat down opposite Hering, took a quick look at what was on his desk: a fax sent from an Italian number, two photos, probably showing the same man, taken about ten to fifteen years apart. The older photo was grainier and showed the man from above. The shot was probably taken by a surveillance camera. The more recent photo showed the man in profile: between 50 and 60 years old, with thinning hair and pale skin. It was probably a police photo taken after an arrest.

"And I was so looking forward to the suitcase full of counterfeit money," Wagner said in feigned innocence.

Hering raised an eyebrow.

"Just kidding. But listen, *Herr Kriminalhauptkommissar*: Before I leave for Italy, I just need to go home and get my sunglasses. How long has he been on the run?"

Hering looked surprised. "You know you're going to Italy? Who told you?"

"Well, you yourself. Apparently there's something more urgent than the undercover operation against the counterfeiters – something that you're taking care of personally. And there's a fax from Italy on your desk with pictures of a man who was probably on the run for a long time but was then arrested."

Wagner tucked her red hair behind her ears with both hands.

"So I assume that the man escaped recently and is now suspected to be in Italy?"

Hering was delighted. Andrea Wagner had the exact profile he needed. He picked up the police photo and handed it across the table to her.

"Simone Noce, born in 1967 in San Luca, Calabria. Sentenced several times in absentia in Italy to a total of over 30 years. And two cases are pending in Germany."

Andrea Wagner looked at the picture, then reached for the older photo and placed both on the table in front of her.

"As you correctly deduced," continued Hering, "we suspect that Noce is in Italy. At least that's where we last saw him."

Wagner was now in a state of flow, a feeling of intense concentration, immersed in the thoughts that came to her while looking at the pictures. In this state she felt free and weightless, pleasantly removed from the world, yet deeply immersed in it. The feeling lasted only for a few seconds but appeared much longer to Wagner. For her, time seemed to stand still when she was in a state of flow.

Some people experience flow while engaging in sports or other hobbies. For Wagner, it occurred during complex investigations where she connected clues like pieces of a puzzle to follow the trail. During her enforced break after that last mission, she had missed being in this state where she could reach her full potential. Now that feeling of fulfilment and focus was back.

She was back.

"And now you want me to find him? How long has he been on the run?" asked Wagner.

"He has around ten hour's head start. Yesterday he got himself taken to the infirmary at Stadelheim prison and then managed to escape last night."

'Ten hours ... ten hours,' echoed in Wagner's thoughts. That was a big head start when you had no clue as to where he might be heading. But it was different with Noce.

That morning, at around 6 am, *U Muto* had been seen at a roadside service station, an *Autogrill* near Saronno. A plainclothes policeman hadn't recognised Noce at first, but he had noticed him because Noce had been sneaking around suspiciously, like a pickpocket looking for a target. In fact, shortly afterwards, at the bar of the service station, Noce had stolen the wallet of a man waiting for his caffè. Just as the policeman was about to intervene, he recognised Noce and, with presence of mind, did the right thing: he let him go with the wallet, followed him at a distance, noted the German license plate of the car Noce got into, and reported the incident.

His colleagues at the *Polizia di Stato* didn't want to believe him at first, because the Bavarian colleagues hadn't yet noticed Noce's absence and hadn't yet issued a fugitive alert. But a photo taken by the police officer was reviewed at headquarters and resolved any final doubts: It was definitely *U Muto*. He had stolen the car from a side street near Stadelheim prison.

'Three or four days at most,' thought the investigator, 'then the Noce case will be closed.' The operation against the counterfeiters could wait that long. Andrea Wagner hoped that the Director of Criminal Investigations would be of the same opinion.

Wagner looked at her watch.

"Ten hours, you say? Who's my local contact?" she enquired.

"*Commissario* Antonio Bonfatti at the Savona Police Headquarters. You're flying to Nice. From there it's about a two-hour drive to Savona. The rental car has already been reserved, as has the hotel. Bonfatti doesn't know about his good fortune yet, but I'll call him right after our meeting ..."

Andrea Wagner noticed that Hering hadn't lowered his voice at the end of the sentence, so she assumed he wanted to say something else. But Hering was silent. He hesitated.

"Is there something else I ought to know, *Kriminalhauptkommissar*?"

"Hmm, yes, well ... Noce and his associates were being investigated by a colleague from the *Carabinieri*. He retired a few months ago, but he lives nearby. I think you should meet him."

"And why?"

"Why? Because Giuseppe Caponnetto is a good policeman!"

"You mean he *was* a good policeman. He's retired now, if I understood you correctly."

"Noce could well be on his way to him."

"Ah, and you think if I get close enough to the cheese I'll catch the mouse?" asked Wagner.

"Yes, something like that. And as I said, Caponnetto knows his stuff," added Hering.

In fact, he wasn't sure how Caponnetto would react if he told him that a German investigator was on her way. Caponnetto was no longer on active service and had made it quite clear that he wanted to let things rest. But perhaps he would support Wagner for his sake – and at the same time he would be better protected than he was right now. At least, that was what Hering was hoping for.

Wagner gave Hering a sceptical look.

"I prefer working with colleagues I know. But if it's important to you, I'll contact this Caponnetto. Let me have his number and an address where I can find him."

Hering nodded, stood up and held out his hand. Wagner stood up as well and firmly shook Hering's hand.

"Wait a minute," Hering took something out of the top drawer of his desk and put it on the table in front of Wagner.

"Take this with you," he said and withdrew his hand. Wagner removed the newspaper that served as gift wrapping.

"In case I don't find anything edible in Italy?" Wagner asked incredulously and looked at the tin of herring fillet with 'in mustard cream sauce' written on the lid.

"No, to identify yourself. Bonfatti will say: 'I like herring better in tomato cream sauce.'"

Wagner looked incredulously at the *Kriminalhauptkommissar* and wrapped the tin in the newspaper again.

"You're having me on, aren't you?"

"Yes, that's true!" said Hering, laughing.

"But what I'm going to tell you now, Ms. Wagner, is really important."

"Okay, I'm all ears…"

"Don't ever order a cappuccino after 10.30 am – at least not in front of Bonfatti or Caponnetto!"

'This is going to be fun,' thought Wagner, who went to the door.

I V

The sun was shining, but it wasn't warm yet. When Caponnetto turned the corner and saw that three tables on the terrace were occupied, he was happy.

It had taken some time for word to get around in the area that the *osteria* had a new tenant. But gradually more locals and tourists were coming to try out the new Osteria Il Golfo. Most guests were very satisfied and came back. A new clientele of regular guests had established itself. Now Caponnetto regretted that he hadn't stopped by more often in the past few weeks.

Giulia had set up an Instagram account for the *osteria*, so Caponnetto knew that lemon risotto was on the menu today. He knew the recipe from his Aunt Antonella's book, which he found while clearing out the house in Pietra Ligure. For years she had noted down all her favourite recipes in that book, and Caponnetto had passed it on to Giulia so that some of her recipes could live on through the *osteria*. The *risotto al limone* was easy to prepare.

In a saucepan, melt a little butter with some freshly squeezed lemon juice. Add the rice and cook, stirring, until the grains are coated. Gradually add vegetable stock and cook the risotto over a medium heat without a lid until the rice is plump and tender, but still retains some of its bite. While the risotto is cooking, fry some pine nuts in a little butter until golden. Sprinkle these over the risotto before serving.

Finely chop some parsley leaves and lemon peel and fold them into the risotto with some Parmesan.

Caponnetto had tried out the recipe himself and found it not only delicious but also practical, especially in spring. He always had the necessary ingredients to hand. Pine nuts didn't take up much space, so he always kept some in his kitchen, and he could harvest fresh lemons and parsley from the garden. The hard cheese from Parma was as much a part of his refrigerator as the electricity supply itself. In fact, it seemed far more probable that a power-cut would occur than he would ever be without at least a small piece of Parmesan in the house.

Just as Caponnetto opened the door to the *osteria* and was about to enter, Concetta came towards him, laden with a tray full of glasses and carafes of water and wine.

"*Buon giorno, Dottore,* just take a seat wherever you like. I'll be with you in a moment."

Caponnetto wanted to ask where Giulia was, but thought it would be inappropriate. It was unusual for Concetta, the assistant cook, to help out with service and she was obviously very busy.

Caponnetto didn't have to wait long before his friend Antonio Bonfatti joined him. The two hadn't seen each other for weeks. They had spoken on the phone a few times, but their conversations had been overshadowed by their disagreement over the wiretapped phone call.

During the course of some surveillance work, the Bavarian State Criminal Police had uncovered evidence that Caponnetto's collision with a truck a few months ago wasn't an accident; it was an assassination attempt – an attack aimed at stopping him and his investigations into the *Agromafia*. After learning about the recording, *Kriminalhauptkommissar* Hering from Munich first notified Caponnetto. But his reaction to the text message that Hering had sent him was completely different than expected. *'Me ne fotte,'* Caponnetto had written.

Hering thought that 'I don't give a damn' was rather rude. He left Caponnetto in peace for a few days and then contacted him again to try and persuade him to support reopening the investigation. Not least because he was concerned that those behind the attempted assassination could be planning another attack. It looks as if Caponnetto had been on the right track during his time as an investigator with the *Carabinieri*. But weeks had gone by and Hering still hadn't gained any traction with Caponnetto, so he finally turned to the *Commissario*.

Bonfatti had always doubted the accident theory. While Caponnetto was in hospital, he wasn't afraid to risk a direct confrontation with the *Questore* in order to force the investigation. The police chief then declared the *Commissario* to be biased and transferred the investigation to a different colleague, who, however, stopped after a few weeks without producing any results.

For this reason, Bonfatti was immediately on Hering's side and had also tried to convince Caponnetto 'not to let the matter rest'. But his friend dismissed it.

"Someone who has nothing else to say is trying to make himself important," was his comment about the intercepted phone call.

"He probably read about the accident in the newspaper and is now bragging about how he took me down."

Bonfatti was just as persistent as Hering, but Caponnetto became increasingly irritated with him every time the topic came up. And even when it wasn't the subject of their conversation, it caused a great chasm between them. Both kept their distance.

When Bonfatti messaged Caponnetto on WhatsApp two days' previously asking to meet for lunch at the *osteria*, Caponnetto was very happy. He had missed his friend and hoped the invitation would be some kind of peace offering from Bonfatti.

'He won't get on my nerves anymore and I can stop by the *osteria* again,' thought Caponnetto. It didn't suit him at all that he needed to ask the *Commissario* for a favour: he wanted Bonfatti to find out who owned the suspicious SUV. While these thoughts swirled through Caponnetto's mind like clouds in a strong westerly wind, Bonfatti came to the table.

"*Ciao* Antonio, great to see you!" Caponnetto rose from his seat and hugged his friend.

"*Ciao* Peppino! My word, you're in great shape – cycling seems to be good for you!"

Bonfatti sat down and glanced at his watch. It was 12:30 pm.

"And you? Are you in a hurry?" asked Caponnetto, who noticed that glance and nodded with his chin towards Bonfatti's wrist. The *Commissario* ignored the question and picked up the menu.

"Have you chosen yet?" asked Bonfatti

"Yes, I'm having the *risotto al limone!*"

"And to start?" asked Bonfatti.

"A small salad maybe. What do you fancy? We can ask Concetta what she recommends…"

"Concetta? Isn't Giulia here today?" asked Bonfatti, knowing that Caponnetto wanted to get back in touch with Giulia, the beautiful tenant of the *osteria*.

"I've no idea, Antò. When I got here, Concetta was doing the service. I didn't see Giulia. She'll be here soon." Caponnetto spoke that last sentence primarily to cheer himself up.

"Then let's not make it too complicated. I'll have what you're having," said Bonfatti, catching the eye of the kitchen assistant.

After Concetta had taken their orders and brought them some water, Caponnetto opened the conversation. He tried to sound as casual as possible.

"Oh, before I forget again later…" He paused.

"Yes, what is it?" Bonfatti asked after a few seconds.

"What do you mean?" Caponnetto replied innocently.

"You just started a sentence and didn't finish it. Something you didn't want to forget."

"Oh yes, it's not that important. It's about a car. There's this guy who always parks his car right next to my driveway. It's annoying! Especially now, when the trades people are constantly coming and going. I thought maybe you could give me the name and address of the owner, then I'll write a polite letter."

Caponnetto added, "Perhaps you can ask straight away?"

He pushed a piece of paper with the license number across the table to the *Commissario*.

Bonfatti reached for the piece of paper.

"What kind of car is it?"

"Oh, it's a black SUV," Caponnetto said in a bored voice.

The *Commissario* was wide awake.

"Yeah sure, I'll look into it."

Caponnetto was surprised to see that Bonfatti put the note in his jacket pocket and didn't call the *Questura* straight away, as he had hoped.

"It's the lunch hour now at police headquarters. It's not that urgent, is it?" Bonfatti commented, on seeing the look his old friend gave him. Caponnetto had no choice but to nod in agreement, especially since Concetta came to the table with their bitter chicory salads.

"Insalata di puntarelle for two!"

Caponnetto pushed the pepper mill and salt cellar aside to make room for the two plates with the fine, elongated leaves that came from the inner shoots of the Catalogna chicory, the Italian dandelion. Their mildly bitter taste, paired with a hint of lemon and small pieces of anchovies, creates a very special mix of bitterness, acidity, and saltiness. From Caponnetto's perspective, it was the perfect dish for spring.

"Thanks. Are you all on your own today, you poor thing?" Bonfatti said, trying to find out about Giulia's whereabouts.

Concetta answered *sotto voce*: "Well, I can tell you. *Signora* Giulia had to go to the bank in Savona today. I thought she'd be back before noon, but it seems to be taking longer ..."

'Maybe things aren't going as well here as I'd hoped,' thought Caponnetto.

The assistant cook withdrew discreetly so she could turn her attention to the lemon risotto.

Bonfatti poured more *aqua naturale* for Caponnetto. To do this, he took the bottle with his left hand so that he could look at his watch as he poured. It was 12:42 pm.

*

At that moment, in the public car park at the Pietro Ligure toll station, the driver of the black SUV started the engine after seeing two black SUVs of the same model turn the corner. The *Telepass*, the electronic signalling system, ensured that the motorway exit barriers opened for both vehicles. It was 12:50 pm.

The car that had been waiting moved to the end of the little convoy, which now consisted of three black SUVs. It would take about ten minutes to get to Osteria Il Golfo.

*

Over salad, the two men first chatted about Juventus' poor performance in this year's championship, then Caponnetto talked about Stefania's move to

Luxembourg, to which Bonfatti commented dryly: "Those born round cannot die square".

"What do you mean, Antonio?" Caponnetto wanted to know, "Of course, I know the saying, but what does it have to do with Stefania?"

Bonfatti, who had gained the impression in recent years that Caponnetto's relationship with the prosecutor hadn't been good for his friend, didn't want to delve into the topic. Now wasn't the right time for that. So he only gave a brief answer.

"Well, ever since I've known Stefania, she hasn't genuinely wanted to commit to anything."

"You mean to me?"

"Yes, that also applies to her commitment to you, and I don't think she'll ever change in that respect."

Bonfatti quickly changed the subject and talked about the body that had been found during the excavations in Albisola. During the early summer weekends, even without all the fuss surrounding the excavations, thousands of tourists from Switzerland and Germany, but also from Piedmont and Lombardy, would be expected on the Ligurian coast.

This issue affected both men. For Bonfatti and his colleagues, this meant extra work – traffic accidents and trespassing charges because some thrill-seekers parked and camped illegally on local property. Caponnetto, for his part, hoped that the renovation of the house would be completed soon so he could rent out his accommodation to some of these weekend visitors as early as Easter. If that didn't work out, the 25th of April – Liberation Day in Italy – would attract many tourists from Milan or Turin to the coast for a long weekend.

It was already 1 pm when Concetta served the risotto. Bonfatti was irritated.

'Today of all days, Giulia has to go to the bank and leave poor Concetta hanging,' he thought, but tried not to let it show.

"And what do you say?" asked Caponnetto, pointing to the risotto with his fork.

The *Commissario* held his right index finger against his cheek and turned it first clockwise and then in the opposite direction: "Very tasty indeed!"

In Italy, this gesture means that the food is so good that you literally want to roll it around on your tongue. It was used more often in the past and reminded both Bonfatti and Caponnetto of their childhood. They had to laugh.

A little later, it was Caponnetto who looked at his watch.

"It's past 1 pm already! Do you think your colleagues might be back from lunch?" he asked, hoping that Bonfatti would call the *Questura* to find out the license plate of the SUV.

"Now let's eat first, *caro mio*. It would be a shame not to enjoy this delicious risotto," Bonfatti replied, and out of the corner of his eye he saw a black SUV turn the corner.

When Giuseppe Caponnetto saw the SUV, he put down his fork and reached to his waistband. But there wasn't anything there.

The movement was routine, but today Caponnetto was grasping at nothing. For over 20 years, his pistol had been in its holster there, that is, when he wasn't holding it in his hand.

In Italy, it was quite common for security detail personnel to carry their weapons in their hands rather than in a holster when protecting particularly high-risk individuals, so that they could react more swiftly. This approach was especially important in Sicily, where these rules of engagement played a key tactical role. But Caponnetto had not been on duty for a while, and, although he was still authorised to carry a pistol, he was unarmed today.

When he saw the second black car turn the corner, Caponnetto was annoyed at his carelessness whilst at the same time thinking through various scenarios.

The *Commissario* had noted the movement of Caponnetto's hand. He smiled and said in a calm voice: "I know it's annoying when I'm always right, but how many times have I reminded you in the last few weeks that you're still allowed to carry a weapon?"

Caponnetto looked at Bonfatti in confusion. He nodded his head in the direction of the convoy of vehicles, which had now come to a halt.

Caponnetto immediately recognised the man who got out of the first car, even from a distance. Caponnetto pulled a face.

"You knew, didn't you? You knew all along?" he said reproachfully to Bonfatti.

"Did I know?" Bonfatti slowly drew his head back. "It was me, Peppino, who informed him. I told him that we'd be here today."

Caponnetto's left eyebrow twitched upwards on the inside. He looked at his risotto, looked over at Bonfatti and then shook his head, annoyed.

"Go on. You know he doesn't like to be kept waiting. Let's talk later, OK?" said the *Commissario* encouragingly.

Caponnetto stood up, folded his napkin and put it on the table. Still shaking his head, he said to Bonfatti: "We'll talk about this later."

He straightened his back and walked towards the convoy of cars.

While the two outer vehicles had civilian license plates, he could clearly see the abbreviation CC on the middle car.

When Caponnetto joined the service more than 20 years ago, the *Carabinieri's* license plates still bore the abbreviation EI (*Esercito Italiano*), as the *Carabinieri* were under the Italian army. But since 2000, the *Carabinieri's* official vehicles have had their own 'CC' code. Now the letters seemed to mock the former *Capitano* of the *Carabinieri*.

Pietro Neri, a former student of Caponnetto's from his time in the *Carabinieri* training unit in Rome, opened the rear left door of the SUV with the special license plate. Caponnetto greeted Neri briefly and sat in the back seat next to his former mentor, *Generale* Carlo Marini. Neri closed the door and got back into the last car.

"*Buon giorno Generale!*" said Caponnetto, still a master of the correct military etiquette.

"*Salve, Capitano,*" the general replied briefly, tapping the back of the driver's headrest with the ring and middle fingers of his left hand. The convoy set off towards the Marina di Capo San Donato, the little harbour in Finale Ligure.

The general looked at Caponnetto.

"I'm pleased to see you, *Capitano* Caponnetto." He turned his gaze back to the road ahead. "We've been worried about you."

Caponnetto replied, "I'm glad to see you too, *Generale*, but I'm a little surprised. Where are we going ...?"

Marini raised his hand to indicate that this wasn't the moment to ask questions.

"It won't take long. I want to show you something and ask you a question. Then we'll take you back to the *osteria* and let you enjoy your *dolce.*"

Caponnetto wasn't sure if there was a mocking undertone in the general's voice.

Fifteen minutes later, the convoy stopped at the Coast Guard car park in Finale Ligure. A *Carabiniere* got out of each of the escort vehicles to secure the vehicle and the surrounding area.

"You have to look out of my window, *Capitano.* Then you'll be able to see it better," said the general, leaning back a little.

Caponnetto leaned over to look out the window. From the marina, you could see the coastline; a little way off, but clearly visible, was the beach of Varigotti, below the Via Aurelia.

"See over there?"

The general held his left hand out the window and pointed his index finger towards the coastal road.

"Have you been here since it happened?"

"You mean since the accident?" Caponnetto replied. "Was that the question you wanted to ask me?" He leaned back in his seat and then answered, "No, I haven't been here since I drove the car down that slope. If you don't have any other questions, can we please go back to Pietra?"

The general tapped the driver's headrest again and spoke to him.

"Tell the *Capitano:* How many times have I asked you to drive me here?"

The driver, who was used to discreetly ignoring everything that was said in the car, was surprised to be included in the conversation.

"You're asking me, *Generale*? Four or five times in the last three months."

"Five times," the general confirmed. "And what did I tell you we were doing here?"

Caponnetto's gaze shifted between the general and the driver, both of whom were staring straight ahead with stoic expressions.

"Well, you said, 'We're visiting a grave.'"

Marini tapped his fingers impatiently. "And what else?"

"You said, the best man who ever served under you is buried here."

That was typical of the general. He didn't like to show his feelings or talk about them, but he always found a way to communicate. Caponnetto was touched and confused at the same time.

"I appreciate your concern for me, *Generale*, but I feel very much alive. My life is much more peaceful now than before. I feel fine."

Marini's bushy eyebrows twitched. For a moment it was quiet in the car.

"Is that the truth, Caponnetto, that you want peace and quiet?" There was a short pause, "Or are you afraid?"

Caponnetto wanted to reply, but Marini raised his right hand. He didn't want to be interrupted.

"The leg shouldn't be an excuse. After what you've experienced, everyone would understand if you were afraid. But do you know what Borsellino said about fear?"

Marini withdrew his raised hand and looked expectantly at Caponnetto. Of course, Caponnetto knew which quote Marini was alluding to and repeated the sentence of the Palermo-born judge Paolo Borsellino.

"Those who are afraid die every day, those who are not afraid die only once."

Marini nodded silently and turned to Caponnetto.

"Here's the question I want to ask you, *Capitano*." His voice no longer had a military tone, but was friendly.

"You hung on for three hours up there," Marini nodded his head towards the scene of the accident, "until the rescue team arrived. Have you ever thought about why? Certainly not so that you could have some peace and quiet afterwards, right?

Caponnetto blinked and ran his right hand over his stubble while the general continued speaking.

"I'm not asking you to give me an answer here and now, but to think about it carefully, *d'accordo*?"

"Agreed," Caponnetto replied, eagerly awaiting the question from his former superior and long-time mentor.

"We know from the intercepted phone call that this," the general again stretched his hand out of the window towards the coastal road, "wasn't an accident. Someone wanted you out of the way. Now that you know part of the truth, I ask you: Don't you want to know the whole truth? Don't you want to come back?"

Marini's fingers tapped on the headrest again. The driver started the car and the escort vehicles got ready to go.

A light spring rain began to fall as they made their way back to Pietra. Caponnetto and the general didn't speak a word. It wasn't an awkward stillness, but rather a reverent silence that Caponnetto would soon be reminded of.

V

Meanwhile, in the *osteria*, Bonfatti had finished his risotto, drunk a *caffè* and the settled the bill for himself and Caponnetto with Concetta.

On the way to the *Questura*, the *Commissario* picked up the phone. That morning, he had rejected an incoming call from Munich as he'd made his way through the crowd of onlookers to his car in Albisola. At first he assumed that Hering wanted to know how Caponnetto was getting on in the meantime, but then, just before he left the *osteria*, a text message arrived asking him to call back urgently. *Kriminalhauptkommissar* Hering answered the call on the first ring.

"Bonfatti? Listen, I have to keep it short. I've got the BKA – the Federal Police – on the other line," said Hering briefly. "Noce escaped last night. As far as we know, he's on his way to Italy. I'm sending someone from the police: Andrea Wagner will be in touch with you. I'll call you back later." Hering had barely finished his sentence when he hung up.

The *Commissario* tried to make sense of what he'd just heard. He took a deep breath and then called Francesca Nobile at the *Questura*. "*Ispettore*, have you eaten yet?"

"Uh, yes. Why are you asking?"

"Very well. I'll be at headquarters in twenty minutes. If you have any appointments this afternoon, cancel them all. Speak to the officer on duty. He should have received a report from Germany about an international manhunt. Simone Noce. Get us the file and start reading."

Nobile was alarmed by the worried tone in her superior's voice and understood that now wasn't the time to ask about the background.

"Understood: international manhunt, the Noce file. Anything else, *Signor Commissario*?"

"Yes, we're getting a visitor, a colleague from Munich. He'll be joining us tomorrow. Please get a workstation ready for him."

Nobile didn't have much experience with international cases, but it was clear to her that if the Bavarian State Criminal Police were sending a special investigator to Italy, it was no small matter. Nobile was curious about the Noce file.

*

About fifteen minutes after Bonfatti got into the car, Caponnetto sat down again on the terrace of the *osteria*. At his request, *Generale* Marini had dropped him off about a kilometre away.

Marini had set too much in motion. Caponnetto felt a certain unrest in his chest, a fluttering in his stomach and a tingling in his legs. He needed to move. The ten-minute walk had done him good, but he still felt restless. Fragments of the conversation with his mentor circled in his mind. He felt all the more pleased when he spotted Giulia, the owner of the *osteria*, approaching him, having just returned from Savona.

"*Ciao* Giuseppe, are you OK? Concetta said you stopped eating and left. Can I bring you something else?"

Caponnetto looked around and saw that the *osteria* was empty. The lunch service was over. The regulars from the surrounding offices and shops were back at work. The tourists, few of whom strayed into the *osteria* at this time of year, had returned to their hotel rooms. Or they were strolling along the Lungomare, the beach promenade, to enjoy the spring sunshine.

"Yeah, hmm, I don't know. No, nothing else to eat, but maybe you'd like to sit down and have a *caffè* with me?"

*

Andrea Wagner was used to packing suitcases and was always very practical. Her wardrobe contained few frivolous items. She dressed casually and elegantly and, above all, comfortably. There would still be enough time for a cup of lemon balm tea, as it took her only about 45 minutes to get to the Franz Josef Strauss Airport. The plane was leaving shortly before 4 pm and was due to land in Nice at around 5.30 pm. Then she would drive in a rental car about 130 kilometres along the Riviera to Pietra Ligure via Ventimiglia.

She had agreed with Hering that she would meet his retired protégé this evening and visit her colleagues in the *Questura* in Savona the next morning. Hering's office had booked her a room in

Pietra for the first night. After that, it would be up to her to make arrangements locally.

On the way back from police headquarters to her apartment in Lehel, Wagner called Hering again as agreed. They discussed that he would call Caponnetto to arrange a meeting in Pietra that evening. During the phone call, Hering repeated something he had already said at the police headquarters, but this time he was more specific. The investigator noticed this. Andrea Wagner had made it a habit to write such things down. Sometimes they were irrelevant, sometimes they were part of the puzzle that needed to be solved.

The suitcase was next to the door, packed and ready to go. Andrea Wagner was sitting in her kitchen. Her teacup was on the table in front of her, and her notepad next to it. She re-read the sentence of Hering's that she had written down.

"It could be that Noce is on his way to Caponnetto to get his revenge."

*

Giulia put her tray on the table. This would have been unthinkable with any other guest, but Caponnetto was now part of the *osteria's* inventory as a regular guest and he was also her business partner, being her landlord.

She had to admit that she had misjudged the man with the delicate hands and narrow chin. Despite all the tension between them at the beginning – or perhaps because of it – she had missed him in the last few weeks when he had stopped coming to the *osteria*.

Giulia took two cups of espresso, a bottle of water and two glasses from the tray. Caponnetto was happy to have company, but didn't want to talk about his encounter with *Generale* Marini.

"And how about you, everything OK? Concetta said you had an appointment at the bank?"

Giulia stirred sugar into her *caffè*.

"*Beh cosi, cosi ...*"

"So-so?" asked Caponnetto. "Well, tell me, what's going on?"

"I wanted to extend the term of the loan. As you can see, business hasn't picked up as much as I'd expected. The renovation was urgently needed, but ..."

"And now you can't pay back the loan?"

"Something like that." Giulia sipped her espresso.

"The bank advisor said the term couldn't be extended, but he had another idea."

"Let me guess, Giulia: He said he has a client who's looking for investment opportunities – not necessarily in an *osteria*, but the bank advisor offered to ask, without obligation, whether this client could imagine investing with you."

Giulia looked at Caponnetto in surprise.

"Yes, exactly, that's what he said. How did ...?"

"How do I know? It's my job!"

After a brief hesitation, he added: "Well, I mean, it was my job."

Caponnetto explained to Giulia in broad terms how the mafia uses restaurants to launder their proceeds from drug trafficking and other illegal businesses. Since there is a lot of money to launder, the mafia is always looking for new avenues. Popular targets are financially struggling restaurants that can no longer get loans from banks. The mafia uses an intermediary offering to get involved in the business, that is, to take over shares, increase capital, and so on. Often, goods then have to be purchased from a specific supplier – initially at market rates, later at inflated prices. Little by little, the restaurant fares worse and worse until at some point the owners are crushed by the interest and debts. Then the mafia takes over the establishment completely. It offers the previous owner the right to stay on using his name – but without any say or decision-making power.

"And just like that, a new money laundering machine is in operation," Caponnetto concluded his lecture and looked at Giulia. All colour had drained from her face.

The contrast between her green eyes and her pale skin made her face look even more expressive than usual, the lines even more striking. With a hint of anger in her voice, her eyes sparkled even more than usual.

"And I, stupid cow, almost fell for it."

"Don't worry, Giulia," Caponnetto gently pinched her cheek. She shook herself as if after a bad dream.

"I'll give you the money to pay off the loan, and my colleagues will take care of the fine gentleman from the bank."

'My colleagues ... my colleagues,' echoed in Caponnetto's head. His cell phone rang. Caponnetto recognised from the ring tone that it was Manfred Hering calling. With his left hand he indicated to Giulia to stay at the table.

"*Caro mio*, what can I do for you?"

"*Ciao* Giuseppe, I won't beat around the bush. I need your help. A colleague is on her way to Liguria and could use someone who knows the area. You would be doing me a personal favour."

'What a crazy day,' thought Caponnetto and said with a laugh, "*va bene* Manfredo, I'll play the tour guide if I have to."

"*Grazie* Giuseppe, I'll give her your number. Can you meet her for dinner this evening?"

"Yes, of course, I'll be here at the *osteria*."

When Caponnetto put down the phone, he looked into Giulia's green eyes.

"That was an old colleague from Munich. He asked me for a favour."

"You seem to be very busy, Giuseppe?!" replied Giulia, somewhat uncertainly.

Caponnetto, who had been thinking about inviting Giulia on a trip to Genoa on her day off, abandoned his plan. Instead, he just nodded and said, "Yes, it's pretty busy."

"Then we should take some time to rest. Thank you for your help, Giuseppe."

Giulia leaned over the table. Now it was she who gently pinched Caponnetto's right cheek.

*

From the *osteria*, Caponnetto walked briskly up Via San Francesco to the house that had once belonged to his aunt and was now his home in Pietra.

A seagull screeched; it could probably sense the approaching change in the weather just as Caponnetto did in his leg.

At first he walked restlessly around the house: through the first floor, through the second floor, looking into all the rooms and out of the windows. Initially he convinced himself that he was doing this because he wanted to check on the progress of the renovation work and the general condition of the house. But then he realised that it was his own restlessness that was driving him.

He paused, took a deep breath, went into his bedroom and sat on the edge of the bed to meditate.

He felt the contact of the soles of his feet with the floor. The stone was cool. Caponnetto opened his mouth, letting his lower jaw drop. As he sat on the bed, breathing, images rose in his mind: the coastal road, *Generale* Marini's face, the truck, Giulia at the table in the *osteria*. And he noticed thoughts: 'I want peace ...', 'those who are born round ...', 'those who are afraid ...' Quietly, he said to himself: 'I want to find peace.'

When he got up from the edge of his bed ten minutes later, Caponnetto felt a little calmer; his mind was clearer. In addition to the question the general had asked him on their drive, a new one had been added – a question he was asking himself. His mentor had asked him if he wasn't interested in solving his case, continuing his investigations and returning to work.

After the accident, he had left because his fitness for service was compromised and he 'didn't want to do things by halves.' At least, that was what he told himself and everyone else. Now the question nagged at him, whether that had been the only reason, or whether there had been another reason, a reason he didn't want to admit to himself – not yet.

*

Ispettore Nobile had first got the workstation ready for their colleague from Munich and then she read the Noce file with great interest. She paused and let out a low, drawn-out whistle when she came across the connection between Caponnetto and Noce. As soon as her superior arrived at the *Questura*, she spoke to him about it and Bonfatti confirmed that he was familiar with this part of the file. At the moment, however, he was mainly interested in the findings of the last few hours.

Nobile wasn't sure whether it was appropriate to ask further questions because she could see that the *Commissario* was emotional about it. After a short pause, he began to speak.

"You know, Nobile, on the day it happened, I was in Genoa for a meeting and was on my way back to Savona. The officer on duty had called me in the car. There had been a hit-and-run accident, a car had plunged down the cliff, and nothing was yet known about the condition of the driver. Out of habit or intuition, I asked for the car's license plate number."

"And then you knew it was Caponnetto's car?" Nobile interrupted. "Didn't the others realise it was the *Capitano's* car?"

"No, and that was just one of many sloppy errors in the subsequent investigation. Caponnetto almost bled to death because it took hours to recover the car. I called him again and again, wanting to speak to him. Later he told me that he heard the ringing but couldn't reach the phone. In the end it must have helped him somehow because he realised he wasn't alone. Speaking of the phone, I should call him. He doesn't know about the new situation yet."

Bonfatti walked down the corridor to his office while Nobile immersed herself in the Noce file again.

*

The *Commissario* was relieved: His friend's voice sounded warmer than he had expected.

"You've got a nerve calling me after the stunt you pulled this afternoon," exclaimed Caponnetto, trying to block out the noise of a passing helicopter.

"Peppino, please listen to me. It's important ..." Bonfatti began.

Caponnetto, whose ears were still ringing, could barely hear Bonfatti.

"If you're calling me because you want to know how the conversation with the general went ..."

"No, no," replied the *Commissario*, "listen, Peppino, it's about Noce. He escaped last night. He had himself taken to the infirmary and then managed to get away.

It seems that he's on his way to Italy. That's why I'm calling you."

'Ah, now I understand,' thought Caponnetto, 'that's why Hering is sending this woman to me – so much for being a tour guide ...'

He appeared outraged to Bonfatti.

"And now you're all going crazy because you think Noce wants to come for me?"

"Well, it wouldn't be an unreasonable assumption, would it?"

"I'm not that special. But if it makes you feel any better: after your little surprise this afternoon, I got my Beretta out of the drawer."

'Well, that's something at least,' thought Bonfatti. "*Va bene*, so it doesn't seem to bother you that Noce is running around freely. Either way, I thought it was important that you were informed. And while we're at it, what *did* Marini say?" asked Bonfatti.

"More important, my dear Antonio, is what I told him."

"And what did you tell him?"

"I told him that I wanted to be left in peace!"

"Well, Peppino, with all due respect, I don't believe you. What with everything that's coming to light."

Caponnetto snorted.

"Antonio, you're my friend. If you want it to stay that way, then stop getting on my nerves. *Ciao*."

Caponnetto ended the conversation abruptly. Both of them felt uneasy: Bonfatti because he realised that he had cornered Caponnetto, Caponnetto because he knew that his friend had said something that aroused strong feelings in him.

Caponnetto's mobile pinged with the arrival of a text message from a German number.

'Hello, Manfred Hering gave me your contact details. I'm on my way to Pietra. When and where can we meet? A. W.'

"7 pm, Osteria Il Golfo," Caponnetto wrote back briefly and immediately received an 'ok' in response.

'She probably just landed and is waiting for her luggage,' thought Caponnetto. He sent Hering a short message to confirm that he had been contacted and would meet the woman that evening.

*

Simone Noce wanted to get rid of the car quickly. If they were looking for it because it had been spotted on one of the cameras installed along the motorway and at the toll stations, the car could lead the police straight to him. Here in Savona.

He was well aware that it was risky to use the car he had stolen in Munich to cross the border into Switzerland and then into Italy. But he had weighed up the risk of stealing another car and decided to keep the BMW until he reached his destination. And besides, he liked the car. He would buy exactly that model as soon as he had sorted out his affairs and had made his escape from here.

Noce turned into Via Francesco Baracca and shortly afterwards drove the BMW 3 into the underground car park of the Gabbiano shopping centre. Even in remote side streets there were always curious residents who had nothing better to do than look out of the window all day and call the police as soon as something bothered them. But here in the underground car park, among all the other cars, the BMW wouldn't be noticed so quickly. The shopping centre was open until 10 pm and would be very busy until the early evening, with people constantly coming and going.

He took the escalator up, left the building, walked along Corso Agostino Ricci and crossed the Letimbro.

This river rises 380 metres above sea level in the hills behind Liguria, near the municipality of Altare. After about only twenty kilometres, it flows into the sea in Savona. Like many of its brothers in the Mediterranean, the Letimbro only carries water at certain times of the year, and especially in winter, when it rains, and flooding can occur. But in summer, the river is a dry gravel bed. Now, in spring, the Letimbro was still swollen from the winter rain.

Noce spat into the water from the bridge. It would take him about half an hour to get to the hospital. Enough time to think about his next steps. So far, everything had gone according to plan. And that was how it should stay.

Andrea Wagner felt the warm spring sun on her skin as she descended the stairs from the plane. The sky above her was bright blue, and in front of her, at the end of the green strip between the runway and the perimeter fence, the dark green leaves of palm trees shimmered. Wagner was wearing pale pink linen trousers. Her beige top was a bit too summery despite the high collar. On the bus to the terminal, she wrote a text message to Caponnetto and then to Hering to confirm the contact.

Ten minutes later, she was behind the wheel of a rental car and driving eastwards on the A8. She wanted to take the first opportunity after crossing the border to stop. She would drink a *caffè* at an *Autogrill* and lift her face towards the sun.

In Munich, before she left for the airport, the investigator had called Volker, an old colleague who was deeply and hopelessly in love with her. Wagner had asked him to find out about Caponnetto. She wanted to know who she was dealing with and not just rely on Hering's opinion, even though she had great respect for the *Kriminalhauptkommissar*.

*

Roberto Papi wasn't the kind of porter who had a friendly word for everyone. Nor did he exude the professional, aloof detachment that some people adopt because they believe their role requires such an attitude – or because they think that this detachment hides and protects their vulnerability.

Roberto was bad-tempered when he was alone and unfriendly in company. Unforced unfriendliness was perhaps the best way to describe his demeanour. This was how he had served as a porter at the *Ospedale* San Paolo in Savona for over 30 years: unfriendly, bad-tempered and suspicious. And because he was always suspicious, over time he had lost the feeling to sense situations in which there was real reason to be cautious.

This made it easy for Simone Noce to make short work of Roberto Papi. He only needed ten minutes to get his measure. Ten minutes that Noce spent among a group of smokers at the entrance to the hospital, from where he kept his eyes on the porter's lodge and the porter's facial expressions. It soon became clear to him how he needed to proceed. You could only win over people like that if you approached them the way they themselves approached the world. Mirroring the behaviour of others was of course always a good tactic for establishing contact and connection. With guys like this porter, however, it wasn't one of several options. It was the only one that promised success.

Noce made it look as if he wasn't interested in the porter and what he had to say. He was dismissive in his demeanour and gestures, even when he asked a question himself. Noce spoke in a voice that sounded as if he had just sipped a glass of sour milk.

Roberto Papi recognised him as one of his own tribe. As someone who understood that of all these conventions and exchanges of pleasantries were a waste of time.

Without uttering so much as a greeting, Noce started the conversation with a rant about 'idiots who park their cars in such a way that they block two spaces at once,' followed by his disgust at the 'outrageously high parking fees' and a lament about the weather – 'now just as unreliable as the politicians.' In between, Noce casually threw in a few small questions. He asked about the opening times, the emergency exits, the access roads for suppliers. He always asked as if it was extremely annoying for him to ask the questions and he himself didn't know why he was even standing there talking.

With every question that Noce managed to press through his teeth, the porter shook his head before Noce had even finished his sentence. Sometimes the porter would tap the table with the overlong nail of his right little finger, like a judge calling for order. Finally, after Noce had all the information he needed, he turned and walked towards the elevator without even saying goodbye to the porter.

If Roberto Papi had known the feeling of satisfaction, he would have felt it at that moment. The man's departure was entirely to his liking. A polite farewell after such a superfluous conversation would have been, in his eyes, a complete overstep.

*

Giuseppe Caponnetto had finished doing his exercises. Since his knee operation, these mainly consisted of regular stretching and strengthening exercises for the thigh muscles: squats for his quads, pelvic lifts and bridges for his hamstrings and glutes.

He walked from the bathroom into his bedroom, looked through the open patio door and tried to work out the time from the position of the sun. He looked at his watch with satisfaction as he picked it up from the dressing table.

'Good guess,' he thought. 'Just after five. That means the midday rest is over and Giulia will be back in the *osteria*.‹

The meeting and the conversation with Giulia had done him good. He wanted to see her again and decided to drive down to the *osteria* right away.

He got out a pair of casual beige corduroy trousers from the wardrobe, put on a sage green long-sleeved polo shirt and slipped into blue derby shoes. Satisfied, he looked at himself in the mirror, put his wallet in his pocket, took out his mobile phone and opened the front door. At the threshold he turned around, went back into the bedroom and opened the top drawer of his dressing table. Inside was his Beretta Model 92 Compact, 13 cartridges, 9 mm calibre. He removed the magazine, checked it and put it back in. Caponnetto clipped the leather holster to his belt and stowed a spare magazine in the ticket pocket of his grey jacket – the narrow pocket that owes its name to its original use as a place to keep train tickets.

In the car he listened to Radio Onda Ligure, a local station from Albenga. *Impermeabili* by Paolo Conte was playing. Caponnetto sang along:

*"Scendo giù
a prendermi un caffè.
Scusami un attimo."*

"I'm going down
to get a coffee.
Excuse me for a moment."

*

When he arrived at the *osteria*, Caponnetto parked the car and read the text message that had been announced by a short ping during his journey. It was from Andrea Wagner.

"30 minutes late. Sorry."

Caponnetto shrugged.

'She's probably stuck in a traffic jam or lost her way. So what?' he thought.

He found the door to the *osteria* locked and had to knock several times until Giulia came, unlocked it and opened the door.

"Ah, it's you, Giuseppe! You're pretty early, is everything OK? *Vuoi un caffè?*"

"No thanks, I thought I could maybe give you a hand."

"You give me a hand? Come on, I can see that something is bothering you, Giuseppe."

Caponnetto twisted the corners of his mouth as if he had bitten into a lemon.

"Concetta told me there had been an argument between you and Antonio Bonfatti. You didn't mention anything about it this afternoon."

"Oh yes, the good Concetta would make a great detective."

Caponnetto smiled briefly because he saw parallels between Concetta and the resolute Miss Marple. The assistant cook was just as persistent, if not quite as astute, as Agatha Christie's character. Unfortunately, she wasn't as discreet as the amateur detective from the fictional small town of St. Mary Mead.

Giulia and Caponnetto sat down at a table on the terrace, sheltered from the wind.

"I had an unexpected visit from a former superior, a general in the *Carabinieri*."

"And what did he want from you?"

"Yes, what did he want from me? Good question. He drove out with me, towards Finale. To where I had the accident."

Giulia nodded. Bonfatti had only told her about the accident a few weeks ago, but she didn't know any details. Since then, she and Caponnetto had hardly seen each other and hadn't spoken about the accident for that reason. She was all the more relieved that Caponnetto was now bringing up the subject of his own accord.

"The *Generale* wanted to know why I had retired, whether I had quit the service out of fear, and he asked me whether I wanted to come back."

"What did you tell him?"

"That I wanted peace and quiet."

"And then?"

"What then? It's complicated."

"Then explain it to me…"

"Well, of course I was scared when I was stuck in the car on the slope, but that wasn't the reason I retired."

"And what was the reason?"

Caponnetto thought for a moment.

"If you're born round, you can't die square."

"What do you mean?"

"I was a good policeman and I never wanted to be anything else – especially not a burden to others. But after this accident, my ability to work was li-mi-ted!"

"And then…" Giulia encouraged him to continue.

Caponnetto was silent, looking for the right form for his thoughts, then shook his head and said:

"Half measures are not my thing, you understand?"

"So you thought: all or nothing?"

"Yes, something like that."

"OK, then you're contradicting yourself."

"Why?"

"You just said that a person cannot change his nature – and that you never wanted to be anything other than a policeman. Now you're saying: all or nothing. So, what now?"

Caponnetto looked to his left, then back at Giulia, who acknowledged his look with a subtle lift of her chin as if to emphasise, 'So, what now?'

"You can be quite tough," Caponnetto remarked, his voice revealing both recognition and surprise.

"I'm not the expert on police work here, Caponnetto, but I believe there must be many ways to be a good policeman. Only you can find the right way for you – whether it's round or square."

She smiled at him. He leaned his upper body forwards over the table and took her head between his hands. She leaned her right cheek against his left hand and waited for his kiss.

Caponnetto's mobile rang.

"Please excuse me," Caponnetto released his hands from Giulia and stood up to take his phone out of his pocket.

Something tightened deep in Caponnetto's chest when he saw who was calling him. He apologised to Giulia and took three steps back. Only then did he tap the green symbol to answer the call.

Giulia, still confused by the sudden interruption, watched as Caponnetto listened intently with a serious look on his face. Instead of pacing back and forth, as he typically did during phone calls, he stood still, about two metres away.

Giulia gazed at the handsome man, her feelings for him having transformed significantly since three months ago. His posture was upright, his head slightly raised. Caponnetto stood straight, but not stiffly. His weight was evenly distributed across both legs. He seemed relaxed and at the same time highly concentrated.

Caponnetto's expression changed within seconds: from worried to surprised, then back to worried. His eyebrows formed a wave motion – they contracted, raised, lowered again and then shot up again.

Giulia could hear him saying goodbye to the caller while he was already moving towards her.

Caponnetto looked at her seriously.

"I'm sorry, Giulia. That was Cristina. I need to go to Savona immediately. I'll see you later and explain everything. But I have to leave now."

He kissed her on the right cheek and hurried off to his Alfa Romeo.

Giulia looked after him in surprise and gently stroked her cheek with her left index finger, before tracing her lips.

*

Wagner had decided to take the A10, the Autostrada dei Fiori, rather than the country road. The espresso in the *Autogrill* Bordighera had been hot and strong. She had informed Caponnetto in good time that she was going to be late, so she felt there was no need to rush.

She was standing in the car park, leaning against her car, looking up to the sky. Small clouds moved in front of the sun. Nevertheless, the light was noticeably warmer and more intense than in Munich, which still seemed wintry. The rays of the sun that penetrated the clouds created a diffuse glow – typical of spring. The light that broke through the clouds was gently radiant, while the sky was resplendent in shades of orange, red and violet.

She looked for a name in the contacts list of her mobile and called the man she had saved under the name Volker.

"As impatient as usual. I'm surprised you haven't called until now, Andrea," said Volker good-naturedly.

"And you? As thorough as always with a tendency to perfection?"

"Yes, yes, just kidding. But joking aside, I found out something about this *Carabiniere*."

He paused for effect.

Wagner bore the tension patiently. Waiting was easy for her.

Finally, Volker gave up.

"Hello, are you still there?"

Wagner smiled and counted quietly to five.

"Yes, of course I'm still here: what did you find out?"

"Giuseppe Caponnetto, *Capitano* of the *Carabinieri*, 43 years old, deployed in Palermo and Rome, liaison officer for foreign services, instructor. He was a big name in the *ROS*. You know, that special unit."

Of course Wagner had heard of the *ROS*, the *Raggruppamento Operativo Speciale*. It had been formed from units founded in the 1980s to combat terrorism, particularly the Red Brigades. Reorganised and with more staff, the *ROS* initiated its services in December 1990 as a special unit to fight organised crime in Italy.

"Retired a few months ago," Volker concluded his report.

"Yes, I know about that. Do you have any more information about the time just before he retired?"

"Not much. For the previous two years he had mainly been investigating the *Agromafia*, setting up and leading a special investigation team in Genoa. Six months ago he had a car accident and took early retirement shortly afterwards.

"Thank you, my dear!"

'There wasn't much new information there,' Wagner thought, getting into the car and starting the engine. She was looking forward to meeting Caponnetto.

VII

As soon as he left the *Questore's* office, Bonfatti reached for his mobile phone. Cristina had called him several times and urgently requested him to call her back. The restlessness in her voice didn't match the pathologist's calm and analytical manner.

The *Commissario* was worried. The fact that he was now redirected to voicemail when he tried to reach her was annoying, complicated the situation even more, and made him nervous.

Bonfatti hurried down the stairs of the *Questura,* hoping to find *Ispettore* Nobile at her desk.

'Perhaps Cristina left a message with her,' he thought.

The buzzing of his mobile phone indicated an incoming call.

"*Ciao* Cristina, what's going on?"

"Finally! Antonio, imagine: it's gone!"

"What's gone?"

"The body. I mean, the body from Albisola – it's gone!"

"What do you mean by 'gone'?"

"Well, gone, no longer here, disappeared from the pathology department!" Her voice sounded shrill.

"Can you come, please?" Cristina's voice breaking at these words. "Giuseppe is on his way here too."

"You called Giuseppe?" Bonfatti asked worriedly. He would have preferred for his friend to be locked in at home until the situation with Noce had been sorted out. He didn't like it that Caponnetto was now on his way to Savona. On the other hand, Cristina Donati couldn't have known that by calling him, she might have unnecessarily put their mutual friend in danger.

Meanwhile, the *Commissario* had arrived in front of Nobile's office and said a quick goodbye to the pathologist.

"Stay where you are. We'll be with you in ten minutes."

Bonfatti went through the open door and caught Francesca Nobile's eye, saying: "Leaving in three, forensics to the Savona pathology department."

Nobile suspected this would be no ordinary deployment. She looked over to her colleague Gianni Sestri.

"Well come on, the boss is expecting us to be at the car in three minutes. And I hope for your sake you filled up the tank this time." She dialled the number of the forensics department and ordered a team to go to the pathology department of the *Ospedale* San Paolo.

Sestri's pathetic attempt to hide how hard he was trying to remember the fuel level amused Nobile. She was able to be quite relaxed about it because she had already checked the tank of the emergency vehicle at the start of her shift using the app on her mobile, so she knew it was almost full.

*

Meanwhile, Cristina Donati had informed the hospital director, who unfortunately reacted as panicked as expected. He wanted to hold a press conference immediately to avoid any suspicion of withholding information or, worse, concealing a crime.

Donati had spent five minutes trying to change his mind with all her powers of persuasion, but her argument that a press conference without police involvement would make little sense didn't convince him. Finally, she had to dig deeply into her bag of rhetorical tricks and use the technique of 'apparent agreement' as a weapon against her superior.

"Very well, *Direttore*, you're probably right. It's best if we hold a press conference. That way you can crush the rumour that our department heads play tennis during working hours as well."

The phrase 'as well' alluded to an incident in a public hospital in Naples where the director had worked a few years back. In 2017, 55 hospital employees – from nurses to doctors – were arrested there for fraudulent timekeeping. For years they had been pretending to be on duty while others clocked in for them. One worked as a cook to supplement his salary, others played tennis during their working hours.

The director had not been involved in this at the time, neither as a beneficiary of the time theft, nor was he suspected of having supported the fraudulent activities. And there were no rumours at all of fraud in Savona, but the mere suggestion by Cristina Donati that this old story could be rehashed was enough to bring beads of sweat to the director's brow. He waved his hands about excitedly.

"For heaven's sake – no, I mean yes. You're right, no press conference without the police, let's wait and see, OK? That is certainly much better."

The hospital director wiped the sweat from his brow with a handkerchief.

"Will you let me know later when you've spoken to the police?!"

To make it clear that he considered their conversation to be over, he put his glasses back on and turned to his computer screen. Cristina Donati left the main building and walked quickly back to the pathology department. Her right hand searched for and found her mobile phone in the right pocket of her lab coat. Now that Bonfatti was on his way, she regretted having alerted Caponnetto.

*

The pathology department, housed in the hospital's annex building number eight, could be accessed either from the underground passage from the main building or through a separate entrance, about 700 metres east of the main entrance on Via Genova. Thanks to the siren, the blue and white police car with Sestri at the wheel made the journey from the *Questura* on Via dei Partigiani to the hospital in just under five minutes.

Right at the start of the short journey, the *Commissario* shared with Nobile what little information he had and instructed her to first secure access to the building upon arrival. He also mentioned that Caponnetto would be coming and should be granted access – he would take responsibility for it.

"It's rather odd," said Nobile after listening to the *Commissario*.

"What do you mean, *Ispettore*?"

"Well, a body is found and then it disappears overnight. At the same time, a criminal escapes from a prison in Munich and makes his way to this region, and the *Landeskriminalamt* is sending an investigator. Perhaps it's all connected?"

"Oh yes, of course," Bonfatti retorted. "That too! The colleague that Hering's sending us, he's arriving tomorrow?" His voice rose to a question at the end of the sentence, as he looked ahead. Sestri saw in the rear-view mirror how Bonfatti was looking right at him.

"*Si, Signor Commissario*, Andrea something or other. He'll be at the Savona police headquarters tomorrow at 10 am. We've already got a workstation set up for him."

"*Bravo* Sestri, good man!"

Nobile bit her lip on hearing Bonfatti's response. To point out now that it was she who had organised the chair and office equipment while Sestri went off to the bar for his second breakfast would be meaningless. Instead, she concentrated on her present task. She would settle the score with Sestri later.

*

Caponnetto was halfway between Pietra Ligure and Savona when Cristina called him.

"*Ciao* Giuseppe, I'm sorry I was so upset earlier. I was panicking because I couldn't reach Antonio. I didn't know what to do."

Caponnetto waited to hear what Cristina wanted to say.

"Antonio is on his way here now. I mean ..." Cristina hesitated.

"You mean, I don't need to come anymore?"

"To be honest ..."

"It's OK, Cristina, I understand. Great that you got hold of Antonio. I wanted to check on my apartment in Savona anyway, so it wasn't a detour for me," fibbed Caponnetto as he turned into a side street to turn the car around.

"Oh that's a relief! Are you staying here tonight?" asked Cristina.

"No, I have to go back to Pietra later, I'm meeting someone for dinner. Say hi to Antonio from me, maybe we'll talk later, OK?"

"Thanks again, Giuseppe. See you later," said Cristina.

At the same time, the police car with Sestri, Nobile and Bonfatti on board turned off Via Genova and came to a halt in front of the red brick building.

Bonfatti went to the pathology department with Cristina. Nobile followed them to block off the underground entrance. Sestri remained outside of the building to wait for the forensics team to arrive and to keep any onlookers at a distance.

After Nobile had secured the internal access from the main building to the pathology department with police tape, she systematically began to question the personnel but without success. No one had noticed anything or anyone unusual. This was hardly surprising, given the hundreds of people who went in and out of the hospital every day.

She called Bonfatti.

"*Pronto, Signor Commissario*?"

"It's good you're calling, Nobile. I was just about to call you, but please, you go first."

After Nobile had finished her report, Bonfatti acknowledged it with an irritated grunt.

"I understand, no observations, no helpful statements – well, good, I mean, not good! The forensics team has arrived now. Let's hope they find something that will help us. Listen, Nobile, there's nothing more I can do here and Cristina could do with some fresh air."

"Would you like Sestri to drive you?"

"No, that won't be necessary. We'll take Cristina's car. One more thing, *Ispettore*: There's supposed to be a surveillance camera somewhere, no idea if it's working though ..."

"I'm on it. I'll get back to you!"

"Great, I think we'll go to the *osteria* in Pietra. That'll take Cristina's mind off things."

"Have a nice evening, then, we'll hear from each other, *ci sentiamo*!"

*

Caponnetto gripped the steering wheel with both hands. The dual-clutch transmission of his Alfa Romeo Stelvio was very useful on the winding road high above the coast. He depressed the lever on the steering wheel and shifted down a gear. After leaving the bend behind him, he accelerated slightly and pushed the lever up again. Ahead of him was a stretch of straight road with a gentle incline.

A lorry was coming towards him at high speed. Suddenly the driver flashed his full beam headlights. At first, Caponnetto thought the driver wanted to warn him about a mobile speed camera or an accident on the road. But the full beam stayed on.

'Maybe his brakes aren't working,' thought Caponnetto.

He folded down the sun visor and tilted his head slightly forward to get a better view. The lorry continued to accelerate and was now being steered towards the middle of the road – on a direct collision course with the Alfa Romeo.

Caponnetto leaned over to the passenger side to get a better view of the cab of the lorry. The man at the wheel didn't seem worried at all. There was no sign of panic on his face. On the contrary: he was grinning. The driver was driving straight towards him and grinning!

Behind the wheel of his Alfa Romeo, Caponnetto grasped the situation in a flash. He probably wouldn't survive a collision with the lorry. To the right of his lane there was only a crash barrier that would hardly be able to slow him down. Behind it, the coastal road fell away steeply. To the left was the lorry, to the right a narrow piece of metal, and behind it a precipice. Then his tires screeched and the metal of the crash barrier made a horrible grating noise.

How many times had he been startled out of his sleep by this exact scene? Caponnetto couldn't say. Nor could he say what was an actual memory or what was just a dream. But this time, something seemed different. No matter how hard he tried, Caponnetto couldn't figure out what it was. Not yet.

Once he got back to Pietra Ligure, he had only intended to lie down for a moment to rest. But he fell asleep immediately and if the nightmare hadn't woken him up, he might even have missed the appointment in the *osteria* with Antonio Bonfatti and Cristina Donati.

VIII

Caponnetto arrived at the *osteria* about 20 minutes before the *Commissario* and the pathologist. So he joined Giulia and Concetta in the kitchen and was watching the assistant cook preparing the dough for a *focaccia*. Traditionally more yeast and oil is used for *focaccia* than for pizza. The dough isn't rolled out, but is carefully stretched into shape on an oiled baking sheet and then left to rest. This gives the focaccia its typical light, airy consistency. Caponnetto watched attentively while Concetta pulled the dough nimbly and deftly across the baking sheet.

After Antonio Bonfatti and Cristina Donati arrived at Il Golfo, Caponnetto joined them at their table. The trio exchanged the little information they had: the male skeleton found during the Albisola excavations had been stolen from the Savona pathology department between 1 and 3 pm.

Donati had been able to narrow down the timeline quite precisely as she had been examining the fabric remnants, presumably from the man's clothing, until 1 pm. After that, she'd first had lunch in the hospital canteen and had then attended a faculty meeting. From 3 pm onwards she had performed an autopsy on another body and had recorded the time in the voice log. The autopsy table she had worked on was in the same room as the refrigeration units.

It wasn't strictly necessary to put the skeleton in a refrigeration unit as it no longer had any organic material that needed to be preserved, or to slow down the decomposition process. But for practical reasons Donati had treated the skeleton like all the other dead bodies that were brought to her. Of course, it would have made her work much easier if there had still been some tissue on the Albisola body.

The pathologist would have liked to have been able to employ her training in forensic entomology, as these methods can be used to estimate the length of time a body has been dead by identifying fly or beetle species.

The dead bodies Donati usually dealt with were quite 'fresh'. Occasionally there might be a body recovered from water, but it was rare to see bodies that had been lying around for a long time where the time of death could be determined according to the development stage of insect larvae. When she registered for the training course, she had been aware that she would rarely use this knowledge. Nevertheless, she was fascinated by the subject and was happy to share her learnings with Bonfatti and Caponnetto – even at the dining table.

*

Giulia's face was still contorted in disgust when she returned to the kitchen. Concetta, who was holding a chicken leg between her left thumb and index finger, nodded to her boss.

"And what does our investigator trio say?"

"While I was taking their drinks order, they were talking about the stages of decomposition of corpses and which maggots can be found when."

"Maggots, well," said Concetta, "if you like that sort of thing. I read that, in Milan, they serve spaghetti made from cricket flour nowadays."

She jiggled the joint of the chicken back and forth between the thigh and the lower leg to find the right place for the cut.

"Is the *Signor Commissario* sure this person was murdered?" Concetta drew the knife through the middle of the joint, put the lower leg in a bowl and washed her hands. "I mean, lots of people die in household accidents: they get an electric shock, fall off a ladder, or slip in the shower and then: snap – a broken neck." Concetta took a big bite of a carrot. Snap!

Giulia shuddered.

"If you want to get involved in the investigation, be my guest, Miss Marple."

She nodded towards the kitchen door.

"I can manage here on my own!"

At the table that Giulia had indicated, the conversation had shifted from maggots to the more important topic of the moment – the missing bones.

"But it's just an assumption that the perpetrator himself stole the body," said Caponnetto.

"Whoever stole the body is definitely *a* perpetrator, because he or she violated the sanctity of the dead," replied Bonfatti, "but we don't know whether the same person is also responsible for the man's death."

"It would be a lot of trouble and an enormous risk to steal a body from a hospital if you've nothing to do with its demise," interjected Caponnetto.

"So let's assume that someone stole the body to prevent the autopsy from finding anything that would incriminate them as the perpetrator," Cristina said, continuing the thought.

Giulia came to the table with the drinks and listened with interest now that the topic was no longer about maggots, eggs and beetles.

"Then we should ask ourselves what on the body could identify the perpetrator," murmured Caponnetto.

Donati considered for a moment.

"There wasn't a bullet hole. At least I didn't see one when I first examined it, so there was no projectile that had fingerprints on it or that could be used for ballistic identification."

Giulia gave the pathologist a questioning look.

"Sorry about our technical jargon, Giulia," apologised Donati. "By 'ballistic identification' we mean the processes that determine whether ammunition or projectiles were fired from a particular firearm. Although this doesn't allow us to identify the perpetrator with certainty, it does mean we can make connections between individual crimes.

"... and these connections can lead to new lines of enquiry," added Bonfatti.

"Exactly, but without a projectile, no forensics – so what else might implicate the perpetrator?"

"What about the remnants of clothing?" Caponnetto asked, introducing that question into the discussion.

"Most of it had disintegrated. I salvaged what was left. The bag was lying next to the body and hadn't been touched."

Giulia looked into three puzzled faces.

"It seems to me that your thinking is too complicated."

She immediately noticed that her wording wasn't ideal and quickly added: "Well, I mean, maybe you're asking the wrong question and that's why you're not coming up with the right answer."

Caponnetto's gaze wandered from Giulia to Bonfatti, then to Cristina and back to Giulia.

"So you think we're asking the wrong question?"

He looked to the side, his eyes seemingly directed into the distance, his eyelids slightly closed. Finally, he nodded his head slowly several times before turning back to Giulia.

"Maybe you're right, maybe there's nothing *on* the body that could convict the perpetrator. The body *itself* is the key," said Caponnetto thoughtfully.

Giulia seemed relieved.

"Well, then you can take a break now and tell me what you'd like to eat."

Caponnetto declined: "I'm meeting someone for dinner later."

Donati and Bonfatti looked at each other uncertainly. It was too early for dinner. Giulia quickly understood and took the opportunity to tell them about a new feature on the menu.

"We're starting to serve *apero-cena*. Concetta has just taken the *focaccia* out of the oven," she said, looking expectantly at Caponnetto. He nodded enthusiastically.

"You're probably thinking that an *apero-cena*, or snacks with an aperitif, belongs in a bar rather than an *osteria*. But there aren't many bars round here that do it well, and I thought, why not give it a go and see how people like it," explained Giulia, looking with anticipation at the couple.

"Then: two *apero-cena* please!" said Cristina, beaming. The choice of aperitif was easy for her. Since the previous summer, she'd found a new favourite drink: Ginrosa. Sweeter than Campari and more bitter than Aperol, Ginrosa is made from aromatic herbs, the roots of medicinal plants and juniper berry extract – exactly to Cristina's taste.

"For me, a Ginrosa and tonic. And for you, *Amore*?"

"Hmm, I'll take a Garibaldi!"

"Nice idea," said Giulia, "no one has ordered a Garibaldi for a long time."

The light cocktail isn't difficult to make, but Giulia liked it because of the perfect interplay of bitter and sweet. For the Garibaldi, you don't just mix five to six cl of Campari with orange juice, as many people think. Instead, you first strain the freshly squeezed orange juice and blend it with a hand blender until frothy. Only then do you pour the aerated juice into a highball glass with the Campari. This is how the Garibaldi gets the typical shimmering red colour that gives the cocktail its name – a reference to the red shirts of Giuseppe Garibaldi, the Italian freedom fighter.

*

Francesca Nobile didn't hesitate. She was familiar with characters like this porter and didn't want to waste any time. Sestri had tried to be friendly, but the porter had refused to give him the key to the room with the surveillance tapes.

"He wants to see a search warrant. Have we got one?" Sestri asked her over the radio. Nobile hadn't answered. Instead, she briskly walked the 300 metres to the porter's lodge and pushed the door open energetically.

"At-ten-tion!" exclaimed Nobile in a crisp military style.

Sestri, who was still arguing with Roberto Papi in the lodge, turned around in surprise and saluted. The stunned Papi also immediately tried to stand up straight as best as his crooked back would allow.

"*Agente* Sestri, arrest this man and take him to police headquarters. Make sure he doesn't talk to anyone or pass on any information to his accomplices."

She had to control herself to stop bursting out laughing.

"But I..." Roberto Papi began to defend himself with a shaky voice, but Nobile cut him off.

"You're obviously obstructing a police investigation, which leads me to the conclusion that you may be involved in the terrible crime that took place here. Come to think of it, you're the main suspect," she said, then turned to Sestri, "*Agente* Sestri, take him away! Put him in solitary confinement until the special investigators arrive. And get the interrogation room ready. I hope the mess from yesterday has already been cleaned up."

It was all Greek to Sestri, but Nobile's military tone had the desired effect. Instinctively he reached for his handcuffs with his left hand and grabbed Roberto Papi by the shoulder with his right.

Papi's face was now turned to the wall, so Nobile winked at her colleague, but he didn't understand her gesture. So Nobile took a step forward and put two fingers on Sestri's hand, which was still holding Papi's shoulder.

"Or can we count on your cooperation after all, *Signor* Papi?"

"Yes, yes, of course. This is all a big misunderstanding. Tell me what you need." Nobile raised Sestri's hand so that Papi could turn around.

"The key to the room with the surveillance tapes. It's best if you close the lodge first and come with us."

"*Si certo, subito*," Papi exclaimed, hastily closing the intercom window and putting up his 'Be right back' sign.

"If you don't cause any more trouble, I'm willing to forget about this and not report it to the hospital director."

"Report it! Me? To the *Dottore Direttore, oh Dio mio*!" cried Papi, clasping his hands over his head.

"I couldn't have known ...," Papi was startled because he had raised his voice in excitement and began to whisper: "Come, come, *Ispettore*, the room is right over here."

Papi quickly went on ahead, his upper body bent so far forwards that his head was leading the way a few centimetres in front of his feet, while his arms swung to the sides.

Five minutes later, Francesca Nobile found what she was looking for on the surveillance tapes.

*

Bonfatti looked around thoughtfully as he sipped his Garibaldi.

"The first thing I'm asking myself is," Cristina Donati took a piece of *focaccia* from her plate, "how did the perpetrator even know that the body had been found? I mean, news about the discovery at the excavation site hadn't yet spread in the media, had it?"

"You mean, it could have been someone local? Someone who buried the body here many years ago and now, because they still live here, got wind of all the fuss?" asked Bonfatti.

"Let's have a think…" said Caponnetto. But he didn't get a chance to finish his sentence. Bonfatti's mobile rang.

The *Commissario* picked it up.

"It's Nobile!" he said. "*Pronto. Ispettore*, what did you find out?"

Bonfatti's expression became serious. The corners of his mouth twitched slightly downwards and almost simultaneously his eyebrows drew together. He whistled through his teeth. He avoided the questioning glances of Donati and Caponnetto by turning away to the side.

"We'll meet at the *Questura*; in 20, no, let's say 30 minutes. *Ciao!*"

Bonfatti put his mobile back on the table and took Cristina's hand.

"*Amore*, we need to leave," and turned to Caponnetto: "Nobile has seen the surveillance footage and managed to identify a man."

As he spoke, Caponnetto's lips formed a thin line.

"Don't tell me she saw Noce on the tape? Is everyone here going crazy now?"

Cristina tried to calm the angry Caponnetto.

"Antonio, if that's true, it's very serious."

"Yes, exactly. If it's true, but it's all just a figment of the imagination."

"Very well, Peppino. If you think Nobile is wrong, just come with us to police headquarters and look at the footage yourself."

"*Pah*, I don't have time for that," Caponnetto replied vehemently, "besides, I'm meeting someone for dinner. And she should be here any minute!"

"Do you mean me?" asked Giulia, who had come out of the kitchen when she heard Caponnetto's voice – indistinctly, but clearly loud and excited. Bonfatti was annoyed at his friend's harsh refusal.

"No, Giulia, I think the gentleman is expecting another lady, one who seems as dear to him as his life." Then he took his girlfriend by the hand and went towards the street. Cristina Donati was just able to grab her handbag.

After two metres, Bonfatti stopped and cursed. The *Commissario* went back to the table, grabbed his car keys and then made a circular hand gesture over the table.

"This is on my friend, he's going to be here longer anyway."

Caponnetto, who wasn't going to give in to Bonfatti, shook his head defiantly and kept his eyes lowered.

Bonfatti said a quick goodbye to Giulia, walked swiftly to Cristina and they went to his car.

Giulia looked after him uncertainly and then at Caponnetto.

"What did Bonfatti mean when he said you're meeting a woman who is more important to you than your life?"

"Are you going to get on my nerves as well?" hissed Caponnetto angrily.

Giulia's answer came promptly.

"I'm sorry, *Signor* Caponnetto, we're not taking any more reservations for this evening. And this," she was the one making a circular gesture over the table now, "is on the house. And now the *osteria* would like to close. I don't feel well." And with that, she turned around and ran into the kitchen.

Concetta saw the tears in Giulia's eyes and bit back all her questions and the words of advice that had come into her mind. Instead, she said, "Let me clear up outside, OK?"

Giulia sobbed, nodded her head, tore off a large piece of kitchen roll, blew her nose and then called out loudly, "*Che stronzo!*"

Caponnetto had already got up from the table and was now standing on the terrace, uncertain, defiance mixed with anger at his lack of self-control.

Concetta looked at him with alert and open eyes. Caponnetto was expecting a lecture from her and was prepared to endure it. He didn't want to start another argument.

"You're not having an easy time right now, are you *Dottore*?"

Caponnetto tilted his head to one side.

"I'm sorry, what did you say, Concetta?"

"I mean, it doesn't seem to be an easy time for you right now, am I right?"

"Yes, indeed. It's not an easy time. Please tell Giulia that I'm sorry."

"No, no. That's something you should do yourself. Just because I empathise with your situation, which is obviously rather difficult right now, doesn't mean I approve of your behaviour."

Caponnetto thought, 'That old girl is as tough as nails.'

The notion amused him and offered him a way out of the hole he had dug for himself.

"You're right, Concetta. It's not an easy time for me, but that's no reason to behave like a complete idiot. Thank you."

His phone pinged with the arrival of a text message.

"I'll call Giulia tomorrow. I need to take care of a guest from Germany now. Thank you, Concetta!"

Concetta said "*Arrivederci*" and whispered "*Vada con Dio, Capitano!*" as Caponnetto hurried away.

Caponnetto got into his Alfa Romeo and called Andrea Wagner.

"Hello, Caponnetto, is that you? The connection here is really bad. I'm stuck in a traffic jam in a tunnel."

"Yes, it's me," exclaimed Caponnetto, his voice getting louder.

"I can hear you and I got your message." But Andrea Wagner only got bits of words; the rest was muffled by a churning noise. There was no point in continuing to shout into the phone. Caponnetto ended the call and wrote three text messages.

"Don't rush, I'll wait for you," and then, "Change of plan. We're eating at my place." The third message contained his address.

Wagner responded with a short "OK" and "I need at least another 2 hours."

After the argument with Giulia, Caponnetto didn't want to add fuel to the fire and take Andrea Wagner to the Osteria Il Golfo, despite the fact that Giulia probably wouldn't carry out her threat and close for the day. Instead, he would prepare a little something at home and perhaps go to the *osteria* tomorrow with Bonfatti and Wagner. And before that, he would visit Giulia to apologise.

With this plan in mind, Caponnetto felt slightly more at ease and his stomach immediately started to grumble. Halfway to Via San Francesco, he stopped off in the Via Repubblica where he found everything he needed. A few onions, some tomatoes, celery, carrots and ricotta: He still had *pecorino* cheese and garlic at home, and white wine of course.

*

Back at the *Questura*, Nobile was standing in *Commissario* Bonfatti's office with two photos. The first showed Simone Noce's face in front of the hospital's main entrance, next to the porter's lodge, while the second showed the same man in profile leaving the premises. However, it wasn't at all clear what he was carrying, but Nobile, Donati and Bonfatti all agreed that it looked like a bin bag.

"He probably got the bag from one of the cleaning cupboards in the hospital. Sestri has summoned the witnesses to the police station tomorrow so they can look at the photos. Perhaps one or the other will remember something that'll help us," Nobile concluded her brief report.

"And you think the bag contains the bones of my corpse?" asked Cristina somewhat incredulously.

"Well, otherwise it would be a lot of coincidences. A *Mafioso* escapes from a German prison, is spotted here in the province and then turns up where a skeleton disappears from the mortuary ..."

The *Commissario* paused.

"And I thought Noce was here because of Caponnetto."

"But one thing doesn't have to exclude the other, does it?" interjected Nobile.

"Good point, *Ispettore*. But I just don't understand why Noce is taking this risk. What's he planning to do with the bones?"

"Perhaps he wants to take them to Caponnetto," wondered Donati out loud.

"But what's Caponnetto going to do with the bones? He's not a dog," said Bonfatti, laughing.

"Not as a gift, but as a warning," said Nobile, spinning the idea further.

"Well," sighed the *Commissario*, "this won't get us anywhere. To solve this mystery, we need Noce or Caponnetto, or preferably both."

While he picked up the phone and dialled a number in Germany, he asked Nobile: "What's the name of the colleague from Germany, the special investigator?"

"His name is Wagner! *Signore* Wagner is supposed to arrive this evening and meet us here at the police headquarters tomorrow."

As soon as Manfred Hering answered, Bonfatti quickly summarised everything that had happened in the past few hours.

"Slow down a minute, my dear Bonfatti. Have I understood you correctly: you saw Noce in Savona and suspect him of stealing a corpse?"

"Well, a skeleton, to be precise."

"And what does Caponnetto say to that?" Hering wanted to know.

"That's just it: our friend is sulking, he's defensive and acting as if it doesn't concern him! He thinks that we're crazy and we should leave him alone."

"But we can't do him that favour."

"What do you suggest?" asked the *Commissario*.

"We'll split the tasks. You've got some photos, right?"

"Yes, two photos from the hospital's surveillance cameras," Bonfatti confirmed.

"Then send someone to Caponnetto with the photos, preferably someone who won't get him all worked up again," suggested Hering.

Nobile, who had been listening over the loudspeaker, tapped her chest with two fingers.

Bonfatti nodded.

"Yes, OK, let's do it!"

"Good, and for my part, I'll call Marini so he can have someone stationed in front of our friend's house. The general has the authority to implement this protective measure, even if Caponnetto won't approve."

Bonfatti nodded in agreement.

"Tell me, how did Noce – assuming it was him – get away from the hospital?" asked Hering.

"By car," answered Nobile, "he stole a Fiat."

"Which model?" asked Hering.

Bonfatti and Nobile looked at each other questioningly.

"A Fiat Panda, why?"

"Old or new?"

Nobile leafed through her notes and then pointed to the right place.

"An old model," Bonfatti replied. "Why do you ask?"

"Noce is clever. When he escaped here, he didn't steal just any car, but a BMW 3. This model is quite common in Munich so it doesn't attract attention, and the car got him to Italy quickly."

"I see," said Nobile.

"You mean he stole a Fiat here for the same reason?"

"Yes," said Hering.

"I'm not sure whether I should be happy that he chose an old model, because that means…"

Bonfatti interrupted his German colleague and finished the sentence: "That he doesn't want to use this car to cover distance quickly, but to move around inconspicuously in this area?!"

"That's exactly what I think. If he wanted to drive to Calabria by car, he would have chosen a newer, faster model. He wouldn't want to drive on the Autostrada in an old Fiat Panda."

Cristina Donati, who had been listening quietly until now, suddenly realised the implication of what they were saying and was shocked.

"That means he's going to Pietra to find Caponnetto."

"That's one scenario at least: It could also mean that he's going to the port of Savona or to one of the smaller coastal towns to get on a train," added Nobile.

"Whatever he's up to, we shouldn't waste any time: we'll proceed as discussed. And please let me know when you've shown Caponnetto the photos."

*

Noce had quickly found the ideal car in a side street near the hospital. It had been easy to break into the Fiat and he put the bin bag with the bones in the boot. Then *U Muto* had driven to a supermarket car park.

He had to wait for almost an hour until a suitable target turned up. It was an old man who had obviously walked to the supermarket, a branch of the Coop, so he probably lived nearby.

Noce got out of the car and shadowed his target in the supermarket. He watched the man take products from the shelves, sometimes putting them back, sometimes adding them to his shopping cart. Noce had seen the sad expression in the man's eyes. It was a look of doubt as to whether the quantity was too much or the package too big. It was the look of someone who hadn't been living alone for long. It was the behaviour of a lonely person – the perfect target for Noce.

At the check-out he had made eye contact with the old man. The man, starved of attention, had immediately offered to let Noce go in front of him. The trap had snapped shut. The rest had been easy.

Noce followed the target to his apartment, waited ten minutes and then rang the bell. When the man opened the door, Noce held a 10 euro note up in front of his nose.

"I think this fell out of your pocket at the Coop."

"Oh, *Signore,* that's very kind of you, but I don't ..."

"I'm sure you would have done the same, er, *Signor* …?"

There were two names on the doorbell, as Noce had guessed. Since he didn't know which name was the husband's and which the wife's, who had probably died recently, he raised his voice at the end of the sentence without mentioning a name.

"Greco, my name is Greco."

"Nice to meet you, my name is Gallo," Noce looked at his watch.

"Gracious me, look at the time! I won't bother you any longer."

"Bother? You're not disturbing me at all. Would you like a glass of iced tea or a *caffè*, *Signor* Gallo?"

As soon as Greco had closed the front door behind them, Noce tugged on the loose end of the clothesline that he had bought at the Coop and that was now tucked away in his trouser pocket. A quick movement from bottom right to top left, followed by a quick circular movement to the right around the old man's head, was enough to secure the noose around his neck. While he held the clothesline in place with his left hand, Noce pulled the noose tight.

Signor Greco made a choking sound. In the hall mirror, Noce saw the old man's eyes widen. Then there was a sound, like a dry twig being snapped between fingers. The crunching, cracking noise indicated that Signor Greco's thyroid cartilage had been broken. Noce pulled the noose a little tighter until Greco's dead body hung limply in his hands.

U Muto dragged the body into the bedroom, washed his hands in the bathroom, carried the shopping bag that was still in the hall into the kitchen and made himself a *caffè*.

*

At home, Caponnetto wondered what he should do first: shower, make the *sugo*, or finish his preparations in the kitchen. He opted for a middle path.

He washed his hands, took off his shirt, trousers and socks and walked into the kitchen wearing only his underpants and a vest. Summer was still a few weeks away, but today it was unusually humid. And Wagner would take more than an hour to arrive.

Caponnetto opened the Radio Onda Ligure app on his phone. He recognised the opening lines of '*Mare*' and turned up the volume. On a board, he chopped the celery, carrot and onion, and added everything to a saucepan with a minced clove of garlic.

When the doorbell rang, Caponnetto went to the window and saw a woman with red hair in front of the gate. She was leaning casually against her car. He recognised her as the woman Hering had announced to him with a phone call, followed by a photo. The music had been so loud that he hadn't heard the car come up the driveway.

Caponnetto opened the window.

"Just a moment please. I'll open the gate, then you can drive the car in."

He pressed the gate opener, hurried into the bedroom, put on a pair of jeans, pulled on a T-shirt and went down the stairs. In front of him stood an athletic woman, mid-30s, with broad shoulders, a narrow waist, red hair, green eyes and freckles on her face.

"I should have showered right away," thought Caponnetto and held out his hand to Andrea Wagner.

"*Buon giorno Capitano*," said Andrea Wagner cheerfully.

"I hope you don't mind that I'm here earlier than I said. The traffic jam cleared quicker than expected."

"No problem at all," Caponnetto lied.

"It's great that you're here, but please call me Giuseppe or just Caponnetto, like most people do. I'm no longer in service, but you already know that, right?"

Wagner ignored the question.

"I don't want to overstretch your hospitality, but could I freshen up a bit?"

"Oh, I was just about to take a shower," Caponnetto blurted out.

Wagner raised her right eyebrow.

"Well, I mean: yes, of course. You can freshen up. It's so humid today, I'll take another shower later."

Caponnetto's face turned the colour of the evening sky in summer.

"I hope you don't think ... I mean, I didn't intend to imply that you and I ... Besides, I have three bathrooms here!"

They both had to laugh.

"I'll get my suitcase out of the car."

"And I'm going to go into the kitchen, I've got a saucepan on the stove. Tell me, Andrea, are you hungry?"

"Oh yes, Giuseppe, I'm very hungry. And please, call me Rea. Only my colleagues at the police department and my parents call me Andrea."

Caponnetto got back to the stove just in time to pour white wine into the saucepan before the vegetables burned. As he opened a can of peeled tomatoes and added them to the saucepan, he wondered what accent the German woman had. Her Italian was good, but she hadn't learned it in Italy, or in France. That much was clear to Caponnetto.

Radio Onda Ligure was still playing, so Caponnetto didn't hear a second car approach the driveway.

The doorbell rang again. Caponnetto looked out of the window and saw a police car from the *Polizia di Stato*.

'That's all we need,' thought Caponnetto, pressed the door opener and only then realised that he had been very hasty and careless. After all, he hadn't even seen who was in the car. He went into the bedroom, took his Beretta out of its holster, released the safety catch, and ran down the stairs. He held the gun in his right hand behind his back while he opened the door with his left hand, without releasing the safety chain, so there was just a slight gap.

"*Buon giorno Capitano*," said Francesca Nobile, "can you spare me a moment?"

Caponnetto secured the gun, put it in the back of his waistband under his T-shirt and released the safety chain.

"Of course, *Ispettore* Nobile, if it won't take too long?"

"No, it won't take long. But I see you have visitors? If I'm intruding ...?"

Nobile had noticed the car in the driveway.

"No, it's fine, do come in."

Caponnetto pointed upwards and led the way up the stairs.

"Come with me into the kitchen. I have something on the stove and I need to make sure it doesn't burn."

"Oh, it smells delicious," said Nobile, meaning it. The *sugo* smelled intense and fruity.

The policewoman opened her bag, took out the surveillance camera photos and put them on the kitchen table. Caponnetto turned his back to Nobile while he seasoned the thick tomato sauce with salt and pepper.

Suddenly there was a new scent. It was fruity too, but also floral, with a woody note. Caponnetto turned around. Andrea Wagner was standing at the kitchen door in a bathrobe. Nobile smiled, stood up and said "Dolce and Gabbana."

"Uh, no, Rea and Francesca, I mean *Ispettore* Nobile," said Caponnetto, irritated.

The two women stood facing each other, smiling. Nobile in uniform, Wagner in a bathrobe.

"She's right, Giuseppe," Wagner replied, taking a step toward Francesca Nobile.

"Dolce & Gabbana."

The scent had been applied many hours ago, and was no longer very noticeable on Wagner, but for Nobile it was unmistakable.

"Light Blue," Nobile added, taking another step towards Wagner.

"*Ciao*, I'm Rea."

Nobile thought, 'Of course you are'.' She grasped the hand that was offered to her gently, but firmly enough not to appear weak.

"Oh, I see. You mean the eau de toilette," said Caponnetto, still a little flustered by the situation.

"Well now, how can I help you, *Ispettore*?"

Nobile took her eyes off the woman with red hair and pointed to the photos with her left index finger.

"Look, *Capitano*."

Wagner raised her right eyebrow again.

"Do you recognise the man in these photos?"

Wagner went over to Caponnetto to look at the photos from his perspective.

"When were these taken?" asked Caponnetto as he pushed the pictures away from him with both hands.

"This afternoon, *Ospedale* San Paolo."

"Is that nearby?" asked Wagner.

Nobile and Caponnetto nodded.

"I'll put some clothes on," said Wagner in a serious tone and went over to the guest room. She thought: 'So Hering was right. You do catch mice with cheese.'

Suddenly she called out: "And what's with this mannequin? It looks pretty battered!"

Caponnetto and Nobile smiled and called out almost simultaneously: "It's a souvenir!"

Nobile told Caponnetto everything they had found out about the theft from the pathology department. He shook his head in displeasure, indicating that he didn't know what to make of it.

Andrea Wagner came back into the kitchen. She was now wearing white jeans and a blue linen shirt. In her hand she held a small package.

"I almost forgot," she said, putting the tin of herrings on the table, wrapped in a page of an Italian newspaper.

"A gift from our mutual friend."

Caponnetto, still deep in thought, trying to make sense of the many questions that Nobile's report had raised for him, said, "Thank you, I'll take a look at it in a moment." He put the package to one side.

"You know, *Ispettore*, I wonder why someone would steal a body twenty years after it was buried?"

"A murder charge doesn't have an expiry date. The perpetrator might be afraid of being convicted," Nobile tried to explain.

"Yes, exactly. But that doesn't make sense in Noce's case. He is a convicted murderer several times over."

"You mean, the risk isn't worth it for more or less one body," Wagner asked.

"Exactly. Why delay the escape and risk being caught?"

"*Dottore* Donati and I," said Nobile, carefully omitting Bonfatti's name to avoid provoking Caponnetto unnecessarily, "were wondering if it might have something to do with you, *Capitano*. Whether there was a connection between you, Noce and the body?"

Caponnetto shook his head.

"I've no idea, honestly."

Wagner's phone rang. It was Hering.

"And Wagner, how are things?"

"I'm here on site."

"At Caponnetto's? Has he seen the photos yet?"

"Oh, you know about them?"

"Yes, that's exactly why I'm calling. Did he recognise him?"

Caponnetto immediately knew who Wagner was talking to. He held out his left hand for the phone.

"Can I have it?"

"Manfredo, listen. I admit, the man in the photos looks like Simone Noce, but he has an ordinary face. It's not proof that he's really here. I believe he's long since gone into hiding somewhere on the Aspromonte."

'Why's he being so defensive?' Wagner asked herself, taking the phone back from Caponnetto.

"Do you think you can sort it out, Wagner?" asked the *Kriminalhauptkommissar*, his annoyance palpable.

"As sure as day follows night!"

"Well then, good luck," said Hering, ending the call.

Caponnetto looked at Nobile. "Would you like to stay for dinner?"

"Thanks for the invitation, but I don't know. I'm sure you and Rea ..."

"Oh, go on, take a seat," Wagner pulled a chair away from the table.

"Hey, Caponnetto, will the pasta be ready sometime today?"

She winked at Nobile and put three glasses on the table.

"Eight minutes," retorted Caponnetto.

He hadn't noticed the military tone in Wagner's voice, nor the irony. He was too preoccupied with other things.

Precisely nine minutes later, all three were sitting in front of steaming plates, mixing ricotta and pecorino into the *sugo* that covered the fusilli.

"As you invited me to stay, I assume ..." she looked uncertainly in the direction of Andrea Wagner.

"It's fine, *Ispettore*, let your imagination run wild. We don't need to keep any secrets from Rea."

"So, just suppose the man in the photo is Noce. This does raise a few questions," said Nobile, continuing her deliberations.

"Firstly, why has he stolen a twenty-year-old corpse? Secondly, what is he planning to do with it?"

"And thirdly, why did he steal the corpse now?" Wagner added. "Why today and not four weeks, four months or four years ago?"

"And what does all this have to do with me?" Caponnetto growled quietly, reaching for his fork and spearing four pieces of pasta. As he raised his fork to his mouth, his eyes fell on the wrapped gift, which now lay in the middle of the three plates.

"Well I'll be damned!"

He hastily put down his fork to reach for the small parcel, knocking over his water glass. But Nobile, who was sitting to his right, reacted in a flash, grabbed the glass and put it on the table in front of Caponnetto. Only a little water had spilled over. Wagner smiled and nodded approvingly.

"Where did you get this?" asked Caponnetto, as he spread the newspaper page out on the table, smoothing it out with his hands.

"Well, the tin is the gift. The newspaper was just used to wrap it."

"Yeah, sure, but where did you get it? You came from Germany, didn't you?"

"Manfred Hering gave me the tin of herring, and the newspaper too. I guess it was meant as a joke …"

"I just had a thought …" Caponnetto hesitated. Nobile encouraged him to continue by nodding her head twice.

"One possible answer to question number three is that he had to steal the body now because it has just been dug up."

"You mean that's the reason for his escape, he wanted to get rid of the body?"

Wagner whistled through her teeth.

"And did he find out about the excavation by chance through the newspaper?" Nobile tried to summarise the thoughts.

"Rea, can you please call Hering and ask if he brought Noce an Italian newspaper and if so, whether he can remember what day and which newspaper."

Wagner immediately grabbed her phone.

"And you," said Caponnetto, addressing Nobile, "can you please drive to the *osteria*? Concetta keeps all the old newspapers for weeks. Heaven knows why, but she's better organised than the city archives. As soon as we have an answer from Munich, I'll call you and you can look for the right edition in the pile. We might get lucky!"

Nobile looked over at Andrea Wagner. In the meantime, she had realised that the woman with red hair must be the guest from Munich, even if her colleagues were expecting a man.

"I guess we'll see each other tomorrow, Rea?" she said to Wagner.

"Absolutely. I'm looking forward to it."

Nobile left her pasta and walked quickly down to the car.

Wagner had no luck at first. Hering's phone was busy. When Hering called back a few minutes later, she explained Caponnetto's theory to him and waited curiously for his reaction. Then she nodded to Caponnetto, to show that Hering had confirmed it.

"He brought Noce the local edition from that day," she said, pointing to the table.

"You must have sent him the newspaper; probably because there was an article about you in it."

Caponnetto rolled his eyes and dialled Nobile's number. He gave her the necessary information. Pause. Silence.

"Caponnetto, are you there?"

He put the phone on speaker.

"I found the edition here in the stack."

"Look in the local section."

"Yes, there it is: there's an article about the excavations on page 23. You were right!"

"Thank you, Nobile. Tell me, is Giulia nearby?"

"Unfortunately not, only Concetta was here and helped me look through the stack. Should she give *Signora* Lenti a message from you?"

"No, it's fine. Thank Concetta for her help and please say hello from me. She helped us a lot."

X

Wagner's eyes lit up. The more complex the case, the more she got into her state of flow. She moved the puzzle pieces back and forth in her head, trying to put the information from the last hour into a coherent order.

"Would you like a *caffè*?" Caponnetto held a Moka coffee pot under Wagner's nose.

"From the good old Bialetti," Wagner said, laughing, "who could say no to that?"

"Now. I won't hear anything said against my Bialetti. It's cult!"

Until the premiere of Bialetti's Moka in 1933, espresso was only drunk in coffee houses in Italy, where steam was pressed through the coffee sieve from above using the traditional method. The Italian engineer Alfonso Bialetti, who came from Piedmont, reversed the principle. In his octagonal pot, the water rose from below through a sieve containing finely ground coffee. This new method and the simple aluminium pot meant that an espresso-like *caffè* could soon be made in almost every Italian household.

Caponnetto had unscrewed the Bialetti and filled the kettle with water. Now he spooned coffee powder into the funnel insert.

"I once read that a Moka makes neither mocha nor espresso. Is that true?" asked Wagner, getting up from her chair. She looked out the window and saw a black SUV, about three hundred metres from the house, stopping and turning off the lights.

"Yes, that's true," Caponnetto confirmed.

"Bialetti invented the Moka, named after one of the oldest coffee trading centres, the city of Mocha, Al Mukah, in Yemen."

He screwed the pot back on.

"The liquid from the Moka has nothing to do with a traditional mocha, though. Espresso and mocha differ in the process and in the coffee. Mocha beans are roasted more intensely and ground more finely."

Caponnetto put the Moka on the gas stove. Wagner took the lighter from his hand.

"May I? I haven't done that for ages! Please!" She looked at Caponnetto like a little girl begging for a chocolate egg in the supermarket and then laughed out loud.

With childlike joy, she pressed the knob on the gas stove. She immediately heard the typical "click, click, click" sound. When she turned the knob to the left, the gas flowed out and she lit the flame with the stick lighter on her first attempt. Andrea Wagner smiled contentedly. Caponnetto nodded with approval and continued his lecture.

"Bialetti Mokas only produce between 1.5 and 2 bar of pressure, which is technically not enough to make real espresso. A real espresso requires significantly higher pressure to extract the oils and aromas from the ground coffee. Depending on the type and machine, the guideline for a perfect espresso is between 9 and 11 bar."

"So the more pressure, the more flavour?" asked Wagner.

"And a nice *crema*," added Caponnetto, preparing two small cups.

A storm was brewing outside. The afternoon's humidity would soon give way to a heavy downpour.

The investigator looked out the window and said suddenly: "So, how do we get to Noce? Do you think he'll come to you?"

Caponnetto shook his head.

"To be honest, I don't think I'm as important to Noce as everyone thinks. If our assumption about the newspaper is correct, he escaped because of the body. And he's here in Liguria because of the body."

"Then we don't have much time before he gets away."

"Yes, maybe just another day or two until he has new ID papers."

Caponnetto looked down at the street where the black SUV was still parked.

'And it won't help to keep an eye on my house or me if we want to find Noce,' he thought.

"So, how do we get to Noce?" Andrea Wagner repeated the question, which she addressed to Caponnetto and to herself.

The bubbling of the Moka was drowned out by a long, deep rumble that ended in a loud, sudden clap of thunder. Caponnetto poured the *caffè* into the cups and placed the Bialetti back on the gas stove. His gaze lingered on the pot.

"Maybe we need to look at it like good old Alfonso."

"What does that mean?"

"Bialetti revolutionised coffee drinking by reversing the principle: instead of directing the pressure from top to bottom, he let the pressure come from below."

Caponnetto underlined his explanation by running his right index finger along the Moka from top to bottom and then reversing it, with the fingertip pointing upwards.

"And what does reversing the principle mean in our case?" asked Wagner.

"Normally, as investigators, we have a body and we look for the perpetrator. This time, we think we know who the perpetrator is, but we don't have a body."

"Because it disappeared."

"Because he made it disappear."

"So we have to lure the perpetrator – and how could we do that?" asked Caponnetto and immediately answered himself, "By providing another body."

"But we can't kill anyone." Wagner laughed.

"We don't have to, Rea. We don't even need a body. It's sufficient if Noce believes there is another body."

Wagner now understood what Caponnetto was getting at.

"So he'll start to doubt whether the body he stole is really 'his'."

"And, to be on the safe side, he'll want to make the other body disappear before it can be identified."

"Yes, exactly, if the body – for whatever reason – means as much to him as we believe, he'll have to react."

While they were drinking their *caffè*, Wagner and Caponnetto played through various scenarios of how they could lure Noce out of hiding. The investigator suggested spreading the word in the media that the police had managed to identify the body in time before it was stolen. However, they quickly rejected this idea because the bluff would be too obvious without information about the victim's identity.

Next they came up with the idea of reporting a second body found at the excavation site in Albisola. But after closer consideration, this scenario also seemed implausible. Not only that, a lot of pictures and videos had been circulating on social media since midday today, showing the barriers and the white tent under which the body was recovered. The risk that Noce would recognise the exact location and that the bluff would be seen through was too great.

"We need to make him believe that he mixed up the bodies in the hospital," concluded Caponnetto.

"You mean, he should think that he took the wrong one and that 'his' is still in the pathology department?"

"Yes, exactly. It's best not to mention Albisola in the media at all."

"And where do we get a skeletonised body from? It would have to be a skeleton for the idea of a mistaken identity to work."

"We don't need a real skeleton, Noce just has to believe that there is one. The pathology department in Savona is responsible for the whole province. We could claim that an exhumation took place in one of the villages in the hinterland."

"And this skeleton was brought to Savona," added Wagner.

"Exactly. Then Noce would have to decide whether he wants to take the risk that he has stolen the wrong skeleton – and that the corpse that means so much to him will be identified after all."

"And when he turns up at the pathology department, the trap will snap shut." Wagner slammed the table with the flat of her hand.

"It's not that simple," Caponnetto said, curbing her euphoria.

"Noce is a sly fox. He'll smell a trap and won't walk blindly into it. We'll have to do more than that."

"What are you thinking?" asked Wagner, looking at him attentively.

Caponnetto showed her the screen of his mobile phone. Wagner picked up her cup and drank the rest in one go.

"That really was a deadly *caffé*," she said, laughing and looking at the time. It was 9.37 pm. Caponnetto also took a sip from his cup and called the *Commissario*.

X I

Cristina Donati shook her head sceptically.

"A press conference tomorrow morning? I don't know how I'm going to sell that to my boss."

"That won't be a problem," replied Bonfatti. "Caponnetto will leak the story to the local radio station shortly so it'll be on the news from 10 pm onwards. The newspaper editors will start calling the hospital director tomorrow morning at the latest. It would be in his best interest to appear proactive this evening by scheduling a press conference for tomorrow morning."

"You seem to have thought it through. I'm just not sure whether we should tell the director the truth; I don't want him to let it slip."

"You know him best, it's up to you. The main thing is that Noce gets the message."

"OK, I'll wait for the news at 10 pm and then call the director. I just hope he's still awake then. What are you going to do in the meantime?"

"I'm going to inform *Ispettore* Nobile, she'll need to take over the night shift – just in case."

*

From the ringtone, Francesca Nobile saw that it was her boss calling. She had just come out of the shower and was towelling her hair. She found it strange to be completely naked on the phone with the *Commissario*, even though he obviously couldn't see her.

"*Buona sera Commissario*, what can I do for you?"

"Sorry to bother you, Nobile, but it's important. I need you!"

"I'm listening ..."

"Caponnetto has stopped sulking and he's working with us again. And he has a plan!"

"You mean a plan to find Noce?"

"Exactly. The best thing is for you to call him right away and have him explain everything to you. In the meantime, I'll let someone in the *Questura* know so a colleague can come and pick you up."

*

Just as a thunderstorm releases the electrical charges that accumulate between the clouds and the ground, some pent-up emotions were released that evening.

Giulia Lenti sensed that she was missing Caponnetto and regretted reacting so harshly that afternoon. She reflected on their conversation that morning and how vulnerable he had seemed. She thought about sending him a text message or calling him, but decided to do neither. Instead, she planned to surprise him with breakfast the next day. First thing in the morning, before driving to the market in Savona, she would stop by his place in Pietra Ligure.

*

U Muto only got through on the third attempt and as a result was angry when his call was finally answered.

"What's going on? Have you forgotten that it's almost time for dinner?"

"No, no, there were just a few problems with the recipe. We didn't have all the ingredients in the house and had to go shopping."

Simone Noce had already called his people twice to find out when they would be joining him. It seemed, he now understood, there were problems with his new ID papers.

"And have you started cooking yet?"

"Yes, just now. The food should be ready in about fifteen minutes. Is that too late?"

"And if it is, I don't have a choice! The main thing is that you remember the chili."

"We've got chili with us."

Noce noted the time. His people would be here in about fifteen hours, so around noon tomorrow. There was nothing to be done; that was how long it took by car from Reggio Calabria to Liguria. Flying wasn't an option: after his escape, the airports were sure to be under close surveillance. Tomorrow, at last, he would have a gun again.

*

Andrea Wagner's interest was piqued. This Caponnetto had positively surprised her, and she now understood why Hering wanted to introduce her to him. At the same time, she felt the exertion of the day, the journey and the change in the weather. She could feel her scar. The high humidity made the scar tissue feel swollen. Wagner rubbed her hand over the base of her pectoral muscle below her collarbone.

"I think I should go to the hotel now. We have to leave early tomorrow and it might be a long day."

"Which hotel are you in?"

Wagner looked at her phone.

"Somewhere in Finale; the colleagues from the State Criminal Police office booked the hotel for me. Just a minute ..." She tapped around on the screen.

"Ah, here: Hotel Casa Magnolie, how picturesque!" said Wagner.

"And where's that supposed to be?"

"Well, here in Finale."

"In Finale? There is no hotel with that name here! Can I take a look?"

Caponnetto reached for her smartphone. Then he laughed.

"What? Is something wrong?"

"Well, yes. There is the town we call Finale, about ten kilometres from here. Its proper name is 'Finale Ligure', but most people just say 'Finale'. Your hotel, on the other hand, is in Finale Emilia, a place near Modena, more than three hours away by car."

Wagner bit her lip.

"How annoying! If you don't take care of everything yourself ..."

"You're welcome to stay here in my guest room, Rea. It's no problem. You can write me my first review on Trip Advisor."

"Very funny." Wagner winced.

Caponnetto grinned. His mobile phone buzzed. He picked up and explained the plan to *Ispettore* Nobile.

Nobile listened carefully and then summed up: "So, you want to use – what did you call it – the principle of reversal? Instead of looking for the murderer, you arrange for a second body."

"First of all, we are only looking for the person who made the body disappear. We don't yet know whether this person is also the murderer."

"Very well, you use the principle of reversal to catch the perpetrator by conjuring up a second body and unnerving the perpetrator…"

"Unnerving him as to whether the body he stole is the right one – that's exactly the idea, *Ispettore*!" added Caponnetto.

"And you came up with that over a cup of espresso?" asked Nobile, astonished.

"Not with espresso! I had put my Bialetti on because Rea and I wanted to drink a *caffè*. I explained the difference to her, namely that with the espresso machine that she knows from the bars, the pressure always comes from above."

"And that was your analogy to classic investigative work: collecting evidence and trying to find the culprit," Nobile asked.

"Yes, something like that."

Nobile giggled.

"So, we police officers are like pumps in an espresso machine — essential for increasing the pressure of the water as it flows through. After all, only with the right pressure can the water properly extract the rich aromas from the ground coffee."

I see you know your stuff, *Ispettore*."

"My grandfather was an engineer at La Marzocco and helped develop the Strada. When the Linea Mini came out in 2015, he had a model in his kitchen before it was officially launched. From that day on, at every family gathering, he would talk about how to make a good espresso."

Caponnetto whistled through his teeth in appreciation, "A 'La Marzocco'!", and continued, "But my intuition tells me we won't get anywhere with the classic approach in the Noce case."

"And so you're reversing the classic approach to the Bialetti principle, in which the water from the lower chamber is pressed from below through the funnel-shaped filter until the coffee bubbles into the upper chamber," Nobile summed up.

"That's right, instead of us looking for the perpetrator, we let him come to us."

"We reverse the principle and work with less pressure!" Nobile summed up, "In fact, just like the Bialetti Moka."

"Noce is too clever, too cautious. We won't be able to catch him on the run, but if we can lure him out of his hiding place so that he has to come to us, then we have a chance," Caponnetto concluded.

"That's a clever plan, *Capitano*! Tell me, will …," Nobile hesitated, "will Rea be coming too?"

"Yes, of course, we're both coming. We're going to bed now so we're well rested tomorrow. Thank you, *Ispettore*, and good night!"

When Caponnetto finished the call, Nobile looked at her phone in surprise and said quietly: "*Buona notte.*"

*

At 10 pm, Radio Onda Ligure broadcast some breaking news. There may have been a serious case of violation of the sanctity of the dead in Savona. A body had disappeared from the pathology department at the San Paolo hospital. It had been exhumed the day before from the cemetery of the municipality of San Giovanni and sent to the pathology department in Savona for examination.

XII

The tires screeched again, the metal of the crash barrier made that grating sound again. Caponnetto switched on his bedside lamp. His shirt was soaked through with sweat, his hands were shaking. He sat on the edge of the bed, took off his shirt and went into the kitchen to drink a glass of water.

"*Buon giorno* Giuseppe," Andrea Wagner greeted him from the kitchen table. She was wearing a black V-neck top with thin straps. Still confused by his dream, Caponnetto just mumbled a "*Buon giorno*," took a glass from the cupboard, filled it at the tap and drained it in two quick gulps. Only then did he fully realise that he wasn't alone and he was only wearing boxer shorts.

"Everything OK?" asked Wagner.

"Yes, yes," Caponnetto looked at Wagner, "well, to be honest, no. Nothing is OK!"

"Nightmares?"

"Yes. And you, why are you up already?"

Wagner put her hand to her shoulder.

"This weather isn't good for me."

Caponnetto had followed her hand with his gaze and noticed the scar between her shoulder joint and collarbone.

"From a mission?" he asked, although he was fairly certain he already knew the answer. The scar was clearly from a gunshot wound.

Wagner stood up, took Caponnetto's left hand and placed it on her left collarbone. He felt the lace trim and a little of the smooth, soft silk under his palm.

"We all have our scars. Some are visible, others aren't. This one here ...," Wagner moved his index finger downwards, "is my scar. It's from a gunfire exchange during a botched arrest attempt. They told us the target was alone."

"But he wasn't?!"

"No, he wasn't. And unfortunately my colleague wasn't as lucky as I was."

Her hand moved away from his finger and moved up to the level of his temple. There she formed a gun with her index finger and thumb and tapped Caponnetto's head.

"So *Capitano*," she said, deliberately adopting the greeting that Nobile had chosen, "now that you know about my scar, you can show me yours if you want to."

Caponnetto moved his hand away from her shoulder and reached for the hand that had just been on his temple.

"I'm sorry. That must have been hard for you. I don't know if I would have been able to go back into service after the death of a colleague."

"What was I supposed to do? Once a policeman, always a policeman, right?"

"*Chi nasce tondo, non può morire quadrato* ..." Caponnetto said quietly.

"What did you say?" asked Wagner.

"Oh, nothing, just a saying: If you're born round, you can't die square."

She took a step to the side, took Caponnetto's glass, held it under the tap and filled it to the brim.

"Would you like to talk about it?" she asked without looking at Caponnetto.

*

It didn't take long for the news item on the radio to find its way into the social media news-feeds. It quickly came to the attention of the editorial teams. The Italian news agency *ANSA* was the first to react. To confirm the report with an official source, the editor on duty called the Savona police at 10.29 pm. Following Bonfatti's instructions, it was confirmed that an investigation was underway for disturbing the peace of the dead, related to an exhumation in San Giovanni.

At 10.48 pm *ANSA* distributed the news to its affiliated radio, television and newspaper editorial teams.

*

Caponnetto was in the shower. The conversation with Wagner, her scar, her story reminded him of one occasion when he had visited his aunt Antonella in Pietra Ligure years ago. Shortly before, he'd been injured on a mission and his left arm was in a sling.

"Peppino, just look at yourself. It's going to end badly for you. What are you doing all this for?" his aunt had asked him, patting his cheek.

"What for? Maybe to make the world a little more normal, a little safer and more civilised," he had answered.

Looking back, he was satisfied with the results of his time in the service, even if he wished that it could have continued for a few more years and that he could at least have closed his last case. Caponnetto had a sinking feeling in his stomach. Wasn't there always one last case, one unfinished manhunt?

When he came out of the bathroom with the towel around his waist, Wagner was waiting for him in the hallway.

"You avoided my question, *Capitano*."

"What question?"

"Well, do you want to talk about your nightmares?"

Caponnetto hesitated.

"It's actually always been the same dream, for months."

"Since the accident? You dream about the accident?"

"Yes, almost always the same sequence: The truck comes towards me. I can only swerve into the crash barrier, the tires screech, metal grates – a terrible, rasping noise! Then I wake up."

"But recently something was different than usual, wasn't it?"

Caponnetto was surprised.

'How did she know that?'

He nodded silently.

"Now you're wondering how I knew? You said 'actually' and 'almost.' A man like you doesn't use words like that just as fillers. This makes me conclude that something was different in the last dream – but you yourself can't say exactly what it is.

"Hering knew exactly what he was doing when he sent you."

Wagner smiled and gently pressed on Caponnetto's shoulders to get him to sit down.

"Shouldn't I put something on first ...?"

"Just sit down and close your eyes."

Caponnetto sat down on a kitchen chair. Wagner came closer to him, stood between his knees and gently placed her warm palms over his eyes. He breathed in and out slowly.

"Just keep breathing," she said quietly. "The scene will come – or not. Don't think about it, don't even wish for it. Just wait and see what happens. The important thing is: you know you're not alone."

Her fingertips gently touched his ears and she felt his head twitch slightly.

"Have you got it?" she asked.

Caponnetto nodded. Wagner let her hands slowly stroke his cheeks before they rested gently on his shoulders.

"And?"

"He was grinning," said Caponnetto, still a little incredulous.

"And what does that mean to you?"

"He was grinning as he drove towards me. That means it *was* intentional. The driver hadn't lost control of the vehicle. I had only been telling myself that all these months. In reality, he wanted to force me off the road."

Caponnetto thought of the trip to Finale Ligure that *Generale* Marini had taken with him, and how they had driven back to Pietra in silence. It seemed to him as if weeks rather than days had passed since then. So much had changed.

When he closed his eyes again, the driver's face reappeared in his mind. Now that he was sure that the man had been grinning, Caponnetto no longer paid attention to his mouth. Instead, he concentrated on the upper half of his face – the nose, the eyes, the forehead. He knew that face. And suddenly he was able to put a name to it.

*

Noce cursed himself for having left the old man's body in the bedroom. Even though decomposition often only starts after 24 hours, unpleasant smells can occur immediately after death when the bowels are emptied.

"You pig." Noce kicked the dead body in the ribs with the tip of his foot.

"Because of you, I've got to sleep on the sofa now." He took the blanket and pillow from the bed and went sullenly into the living room.

After a few hours of fitful sleep, *U Muto* took a cold shower at around 6.45 am. To start the day, he wanted to prepare a hearty *frittata* using what was in the fridge.

For a perfect Italian omelette, the eggs must first be carefully whisked so that the mixture is even and fluffy. A little splash of milk or cream can help the *frittata* to end up particularly light, but too much liquid can make the *frittata* heavy and dense instead of giving it the desired airiness. While whisking the mixture, you can season it with a little salt, freshly ground pepper and, depending on your taste, chopped herbs such as parsley, chives or basil. Even seasoning ensures the flavours are distributed harmoniously.

Noce's *frittata* consisted of three eggs, half a pepper that was no longer quite fresh, onions, two small tomatoes and some leftover pecorino cheese that he grated. There was no milk or cream in the house.

While he waited for the pan to heat up, Noce turned on the kitchen radio – just in time for the 7 am news. He couldn't believe what he was hearing.

*

Today was a good day for the fishermen casting out their lines on the beach at Pietra. A gentle, not too strong wind blew in from the mountains across the coast towards the sea. The sky was overcast; there would probably be some rain later.

"I wonder what he did with the body?"

Wagner stood next to Caponnetto in front of her car.

"Is it significant, or is it just a distraction?"

"Well, I think it does make a difference whether he just threw the bones in the nearest bin or 'laid them to rest' somewhere else," Wagner made air quotation marks with her hands.

"That leads to the real question: Why is the body so important to Noce?"

"Well, maybe it's someone who meant a lot to him."

"Or he wanted to prevent us from identifying the dead man?"

"Yes, but what about the body would be so dangerous for him? He's been convicted of murder several times over. Even if we could prove from the body that he had committed another murder, why take this risk? Why make a poorly planned escape from a German prison and then travel to Italy alone? Why expose yourself to the risk of being discovered and then steal a body that is just one of many victims he has on his conscience."

Caponnetto got into his car and rolled down the window.

"I don't think we'll know until we catch Noce."

He tapped the car door from the outside with the flat of his left hand and then crossed his middle and index fingers.

"That's if he's willing to talk to us."

The two had briefly discussed how they should split up. Wagner had insisted on driving to the *Questura* alone early in the morning and having a classic Italian breakfast in a bar on the way there: cappuccino and brioche.

Being a good host, Caponnetto had naturally offered to have breakfast with her and then accompany her to the *Questura*. Wagner had politely refused. He graciously repeated his offer and after she turned it down once more, he decided that Wagner should have her own experience.

Caponnetto also left the house in Pietra without breakfasting and headed to his apartment at the port of Savona. There he would shower and have breakfast in the bar by the marina. He had a few things to take care of in Savona and yes, of course he wanted to be close to the *Questura* – just in case.

*

The first part of Andrea Wagner's plan worked, even if she couldn't immediately decide which filling to choose for her brioche: pistachio, vanilla, chocolate or apricot jam.

She watched the barista while he prepared the cappuccino. He tilted the cup slightly and placed the milk jug close to the surface of the espresso. Starting in the middle, he poured the milk slowly and evenly. As soon as the foam began to float on the surface, he lifted the jug slightly and then poured faster. With a light, circular movement, the foam spread out into a round pattern. Just before the end, the barista drew the jug back through the middle with a quick movement, forming a heart.

In contrast, her start at the *Questura*, didn't go quite as planned. The entrance gate was opened for her, but she was denied access to the non-public area of the police headquarters. The officer on duty looked at the woman with red hair, looked at the book in front of him, then back again at Wagner and shook his head.

If the two had been standing in front of each other in a restaurant, his words would have been: 'I'm sorry, madam, unfortunately we don't have a reservation for Ms Wagner for this evening, and what's more, we won't be accepting reservations until July 2028.' Meanwhile, the young police officer in the Savona *Questura* simply said, "I can´t find you here in my list *Signora*. You'll have to take a seat in the waiting room."

"And for how long?" asked Wagner as she put her ID card back in her pocket.

"Until someone comes to identify and register you as a visitor, *Signora*."

"Nobile, you must know your colleague Nobile? And Bonfatti! Bonfatti must be your superior. Both have been informed! They know I'm coming. They're expecting me!" Wagner exclaimed.

The officer on duty silently stretched out his right arm.

"Please, *Signora* ..."

Wagner briefly debated whether to show the officer on duty the weapon holstered above the right back pocket of her jeans but ultimately decided against it, uncertain of how the young policeman might react.

Triggering an active shooter alert at Savona police headquarters at 7 in the morning was not something she could report to *Kriminalhauptkommissar* Hering in Munich as a milestone of a successful mission. The thought amused her, however, which in turn helped her to relax.

She would wait until Nobile or Bonfatti came to the *Questura*, which – she hoped – wouldn't take too long.

The German investigator couldn't have known that Nobile had been picked up from her home very early that day by a patrol car that had taken her to Stella San Giovanni. The small village was about fifteen kilometres inland from Savona, 260 metres above sea level in the Ligurian Apennines, the north-western end of the Apennines in Italy. Bonfatti had stayed overnight with Cristina Donati in Varigotti and had been assigned to shooting practice this morning, so he too wouldn't be arriving at the police station until after 10 am. If the officer on duty had made a little more effort and taken the visitor's request more seriously, he would have realised this.

XIII

"Did you know, *Commissario*, that Sandro Pertini is buried in this cemetery?"

Bonfatti, who had called Nobile but was still thinking about arranging dinner at the Osteria Il Golfo – it was his and Cristina Donati's anniversary today – asked absentmindedly: "In Pietra Ligure?"

"Why Pietra Ligure? No, in Stella San Giovanni. The President of the Republic is buried there ..."

"Ah, really? Is Pertini buried there?"

"Si, *Signor Commissario*, I went to school in Savona. There isn't a schoolchild here who hasn't been to the *Museo* Sandro Pertini at least once."

"Well, I knew he wasn't buried in Rome, but I had no idea that Pertini was buried in San Giovanni."

In 1983, the Italian singer Toto Cutugno mentioned Sandro Pertini in the second verse of his song *L'italiano*: *'Un partigiano come presidente'* refers to Pertini, who fought as a partisan in the resistance against the fascists and was one of the leaders of the National Liberation Committee for Northern Italy.

When, after 16 ballots, Pertini was elected head of state of the Italian Republic in 1978 at the age of over 80, no one suspected that he would become one of the country's most popular presidents. Although he remained in office until 1985, it seems that there are only two photographs from his seven-year term. From 1982 onwards, newspapers and television almost exclusively showed one of two images whenever there was a news story about Pertini.

One photo captured him in a blue suit, beaming with joy, his hands raised as if bestowing blessings and congratulations upon the pitch below. He's holding his pipe in his left hand, and the Spanish King Juan Carlos is standing next to him. This photo was taken on July 11, 1982 at the Estadio Santiago Bernabéu in Madrid, shortly after Italy had won the World Cup final 3-1 against Germany.

The other photo, published by the presidential administration as the official portrait of his term in office, also shows Pertini with a pipe in his left hand. Behind him, golden ornaments and a blue-patterned wall decoration set the scene, while in the foreground, Pertini appears with a serious expression behind the tinted lenses of his horn-rimmed glasses. This photo was taken in the Palazzo del Quirinale, the official residence of the Italian President.

Bonfatti thought of this picture of Sandro Pertini and focused his thoughts. Now he understood why this short excursion into Italy's political history was important.

"*Brava* Nobile! A very good idea!"

"Thank you, *Signor Commissario*! Will you inform the *Capitano* and the lady from Germany?" asked Nobile.

"Lady from Germany? I don't quite understand, *Ispettore*," replied the *Commissario*.

"I thought we were going to meet this Andrea Wagner later in the *Questura* – is he bringing anyone else from Germany with him?"

It was only then that Francesca Nobile realised that no one had informed the *Commissario* that the special investigator from Germany, Andrea Wagner, was not a man but a woman.

"The best thing to do is call the *Capitano*, *Signor Commissario*. I think he has more information about our visitor from Germany."

Bonfatti scratched his head thoughtfully and dialled Caponnetto's number. His friend answered on the hands-free system.

"*Ciao* Antonio. What's up?"

"You tell me!"

"What do you mean?"

"Nobile said you had contact with the special investigator from Germany."

"Yes, Hering put us in touch. I met her yesterday."

"You? We are talking about the same person, aren't we? Andrea Wagner, a special investigator with the Bavarian State Criminal Police!"

"Yes, in Germany, Andrea is a woman's name, unlike in Italy where it's a man's name."

"OK, *capito*, and where is this Andrea now?"

"Well, I thought she was with you in the *Questura*," retorted Caponnetto, mischievously.

"*Porca miseria*, I'm not even at the police station yet – and Nobile went straight to the cemetery. I'm going to call the officer on duty right away, he probably just put our colleague in the waiting room without informing me."

"Yes, that's exactly what he did. She called me and I told her that the *Commissario* was probably still sleeping off his hangover from last night and that she should go straight to Stella San Giovanni to meet Nobile there."

"Well, that's just great," Bonfatti jumped up.

"I'm lost for words!! Are you in charge of the tactical operational planning now? Or are you back on duty and I hadn't been informed yet?"

"*Scusa* Antonio. 'Once a policeman, always a policeman.' But you're right, I should have conferred with you first."

"Never mind, you said the special investigator is on her way to the cemetery. That's good!"

Caponnetto was surprised by Bonfatti's quick change of mood.

"Why is that good?"

"Pertini!"

"What?"

"Sandro Pertini is buried in the San Giovanni cemetery."

"And?"

"If this Wagner woman is in the cemetery and Noce turns up and becomes suspicious, or one of his people is snooping around... if he sends them ahead..."

"What then?" asked Caponnetto, who was getting impatient because he had been waiting at a red light for what felt like ten minutes.

"Then she should speak to Noce or his accomplices directly and ask the way to the President's grave. Don't you understand? She won't arouse any suspicion!"

"Well, Antonio, I don't know..."

"Man, Peppino, you *are* rusty. *Un po´ di fantasia!* She should just say she's from the German television and doing some research for a documentary or something like that."

Finally the light turned green.

"Listen, Antonio, do you remember Domenico Condello?"

"From Reggio Calabria? Yes, of course. You arrested him a few months ago when he took delivery of a container of olives at the port. I think it was from Tunisia ... it was shortly before your accident."

"The shipment came from Morocco, but it was this Condello I'm referring to. The olives were to be re-labelled as "Made in Italy" and then processed into oil."

"What about Condello? Why are you asking?"

"Was he convicted?" asked Caponnetto.

"You don't know? No charges were ever brought. The case was dropped and Condello was released from custody. I don't remember exactly when, but it must be ..."

"Please look it up. I bet it was the day of my accident or the day before. And please also look up which prosecutor handled the case.

"I don't have to look that up. It was Lombardo, that arsehole! The same one who stopped the investigation into your accident." Bonfatti was upset. Just thinking about Umberto Lombardo made the veins in his neck bulge.

"You still haven't told me why you've rekindled your interest in Domenico Condello right now."

"I'm pretty sure it was Condello who was driving the truck back then." With these words, Caponnetto ended the conversation.

He tried to remember when he had last encountered prosecutor Lombardo. Umberto Lombardo, in his late thirties, was a gaunt man who often said *'prima di adesso.*' This was an unusual variation on the already antiquated phrase '*prima di ora*', meaning 'before this point in time'.

For example, when Lombardo wanted to say that a suspect had not been conspicuous until now, he would say: 'The perpetrator hadn't been conspicuous before this point in time.' This old-fashioned way of speaking didn't match his actual age, but Lombardo looked prematurely old and grey anyway. At the same time, though, he always dressed in a decidedly youthful and modern manner, which highlighted the incongruity and made him seem even more eccentric.

Caponnetto and the *Commissario* had agreed that Gianni Sestri and Bonfatti would wait at the post office on Corso Tardy e Benech. The boulevard, named after the freedom fighters Jacopo Tardy and Giuseppe Benech, was tactically a good place to wait. This was this intersection of the SS1 and SP29 and would allow them to quickly set off in either direction once they knew Noce's location. Caponnetto was to park his Alfa Romeo Stelvio there and meet up with Bonfatti and Sestri.

*

Sestri almost lost his appetite when he heard that he would be seeing Giuseppe Caponnetto again. After all, it was Sestri who was ultimately responsible for the many derogatory newspaper reports after Caponnetto – a retired *Carabiniere*, of all people – helped the *Polizia di Stato* solve a homicide case. After the murderer had confessed, Sestri happened to meet a journalist in the bar where he had his breakfast every day, purely by chance, as Sestri had naively assumed.

The journalist had invited the policeman to a piece of *focaccia*, praised the excellent investigative work of the Savona police and skilfully engaged Sestri in conversation. Between two bites of *focaccia*, Sestri then blurted out Caponnetto's involvement, although the *Questura* had agreed not to mention this detail in the official reports. Caponnetto was happy that his role in solving the Umberto Serra case was not made public. So it was all the more annoying for him when one newspaper after another picked up the story and even asked him for an interview.

Bonfatti, who for his part had to explain himself to the police chief, immediately suspected *Agente* Sestri and took him to task. The latter stubbornly denied it and in the days that followed only spoke in the *Questura* when it was absolutely unavoidable.

After three days, *Ispettore* Nobile suggested using very special, enhanced interrogation techniques on Sestri. The next morning, she brought a *panino* with tomatoes, mozzarella and grilled aubergine, already cut in half. She placed it on the very edge of her desk, close to Sestri's seat. It took less than two minutes for him to give in.

"That smells absolutely delicious, Francesca. Did you get it from the bar in the shopping centre?"

"No, what are you thinking, Gianni! Have you ever seen such a delicious *panino* in the Gabbiano?"

"Uh, no, that's exactly why I'm asking ..."

"This *panino*," Nobile tapped the half-open bag lightly with her index finger, "this *panino* is from the Topolino bar. I made a special detour for it this morning."

She took one half in both hands and held the panino under her nose. "Mmmmmhh, it smells delicious!"

Sestri watched his colleague with his mouth half open as she bit into the *panino*. It almost seemed as if he was unconsciously making chewing movements.

"Gianni, would you like a piece too?"

She held out the bag with the other half, but jerked it back again when Sestri held out his left hand.

"The bad mood here in the *Questura* is rather depressing, don't you think?" she said and pulled back her hand with the bag a little further.

Sestri, who knew what his colleague was alluding to, fidgeted embarrassedly, while his hand remained stretched out in the air, like the girl in the Banksy painting.

"Well, everything will calm down again – I hope," he added sheepishly, "I didn't mean it."

Francesca Nobile handed him the *panino* and *Commissario* Bonfatti gave him a lecture for dessert and warned him that if he ever stepped out of line again he would recommend that Sestri be transferred to Vernazza or Riomaggiore.

"Then you can experience the most beautiful side of Liguria, the legendary Cinque Terre!" laughed the *Commissario*.

"Five kitschy villages, gaudily painted and masses of tourists, as well as those narrow, steep streets. You'll see, after a few weeks of patrolling up and down hills you'll feel like you've been reborn. Especially since the inflated prices will quickly make you lose your appetite. You'll be able to box as a lightweight at the next police championships."

The thought of soon being in the patrol car with Caponnetto and Bonfatti again brought back unpleasant memories of this episode for Gianni Sestri, as he feared that Caponnetto might still be angry with him. But his worries were unfounded – neither his superior nor Caponnetto were inclined to bear a grudge.

*

At the same time, Wagner called Nobile to tell her that she would be arriving in about ten minutes. She liked Nobile's suggestion to disguise herself as a journalist.

A little later, Wagner stopped her car in the car park in front of the church of San Giovanni Battista. She knew that Nobile and a colleague had taken up position in the bell tower. From there they had a view of large parts of the grounds, but Wagner now realised that there were two blind spots.

Diagonally opposite the church, a sign advertised a Bed and Breakfast. Wagner decided to take up position there and parked the car backwards into the driveway so that she had a good view of the entrance to the churchyard. She held her mobile to her ear to give the impression that she was talking on the phone.

Through her rear-view mirror, Wagner saw the door of the Bed and Breakfast open. She watched the person stepping out onto the street and tried to assess whether she posed a threat.

'Early thirties; about 1.60 m tall; around 58 or maybe only 54 kilos; blond, shoulder-length hair; dark blue knee-length sleeveless dress, not suitable for this time of year.'

Satisfied with herself and her powers of observation, Wagner began to answer her imaginary conversation partner on the phone.

"Yes, exactly, probably in a few days. It depends on how quickly I finish my assignment here."

The woman in the dark blue dress knocked on the window of the driver's door. Wagner kept talking and said loudly in German: "Wait a minute. No, it's better if I call back." She put her mobile on the passenger seat and opened the window.

"Buon giorno. These parking spaces are only for guests of the *cassetta.* Could you please drive on?" asked the woman in a polite but firm tone.

"Buon giorno, Signora. I was hoping to stay here for a night or two. Do you have a room available?"

"Mi dispiace, so sorry. We're closed. It's not worth opening at this time of year as we don't have enough guests."

The investigator pointed to her bare arms.

"But you are expecting it to get a bit warmer today?"

The young woman immediately understood what she meant.

"No, it'll stay cool today and probably for the next few days too. We're doing a photo shoot for our Facebook and Instagram accounts to advertise when the season starts."

"Ah, and in the summer you won't have time for photos because there's so much going on? So you're already taking some pictures that look like summer?!"

The hotel owner liked this woman with red hair who had started a casual conversation so easily and unobtrusively. She thought about showing her the rooms.

'Who knows how many people she could tell about us ...?' she asked herself, but then she just said, "You're from Germany, aren't you?"

"Yes, that's right."

"And what brings you to this area? There's hardly anything going on here at the moment."

"Oh, I'm here on business. I work as a journalist and I'm researching a documentary about Sandro Pertini."

While Wagner was answering the woman, she noticed out of the corner of her eye that the priest was leaving the church accompanied by a man.

"Tell me, how far is it to the cemetery?"

"It's not far, about 200 metres down the road. You're welcome to leave the car here. You won't be staying here forever, will you?" The woman giggled, thinking of the allusion to the cemetery and eternal resting place.

"There's not that much to see. It's a family grave like many others in the cemetery, except that the Pertini grave has a Tricolour flag."

Wagner thanked her and considered whether she should go on ahead or wait until the priest and his companion had walked a little way down the street.

But the woman made the decision for Wagner. She waved in the direction of the two men and called out: "*Buon giorno, Padre* Larusso. The *Signora* wants to visit the *tomba* Pertini. You're going over to the cemetery, aren't you? Perhaps you can show her the way!?"

Wagner got out of the car and thanked her.

"Very kind of you. I'll let you know when I leave."

"Yes, of course. Then I can show you the rooms. Maybe you'd like to come back when we're open."

The priest waved Andrea Wagner over and stopped with his companion on the other side of the street.

Wagner was in no doubt: She was looking into the dark eyes of Simone Noce. The investigator held up her mobile phone and took a selfie. It was the signal she'd agreed with Nobile that she had identified Noce. Nobile would now climb down the steep stairs of the bell tower, enter the cemetery through the back entrance and wait for her at the meeting point.

"*Buon giorno.* You want to go to the president's grave? That's good! There aren't many visitors anymore. The last time there was a big crowd here was in 2017. Everything was full of police and *Carabinieri*."

'Did Noce just twitch or did I just imagine it?' Wagner thought. She would try to put Noce under more pressure, so she probed further, staring at his pupils.

"And now there are probably a lot of police here again, right? I mean because of the exhumation and the disturbance of the corpse in Savona. I read about it in the newspaper. A terrible business!"

Wagner saw exactly how Noce's pupils dilated. He was stressed – and that was good! When someone is under stress, their perception, risk-taking and self-control change.

A stressed Noce would be less attentive, act more carelessly and could be more easily taken by surprise. However, he might also react very impulsively. So it was advisable to be cautious.

Father Larusso cleared his throat to indicate that he was uncomfortable with the subject of the exhumation. This was the reason why his companion had come to see him. The man had explained that he wanted to pray for the peace of his old friend's soul at the empty grave.

The plan that Wagner, Bonfatti and Caponnetto had worked on through multiple iterations was working.

They had looked for a cemetery in the province of Savona where a grave had recently been opened so that the story of the exhumation and the mix-up in the hospital would be credible.

As luck would have it, a man's body had been exhumed from the place where the President of the Republic was buried. But contrary to what the media suggested, this wasn't to do with a criminal investigation, but for a family reunion. The man's remains had been on their way to France since yesterday. *Padre* Larusso, who attended the exhumation and had been let in on the plan by Nobile, played his part masterfully in their little charade.

Completely unexpectedly, the investigator heard Simone Noce's thin, reedy voice of for the first time.

"Tell me, don't we know each other? I could swear we've met before."

"Oh, I hear that often. I have such an ordinary face. No, I don't believe we've met before. My name is Meier, Silvia Meier."

When the trio reached the entrance to the cemetery, Noce was still wondering where he had seen this Ms. Meier before.

"So, *Signora* Meier. Just follow the main path, the President's grave is on the left. You can't miss it ..."

"Because of the flag," added Wagner.

The priest nodded.

"*Sì*, because of the *bandiera*."

"*Grazie, Padre*."

Wagner looked Noce straight in the eye and said, "Goodbye. All the best for you, and don't think too hard about where you've seen me before. That's what gives you wrinkles."

'Let him get nervous,' thought Wagner, 'maybe then he'll make a mistake.'

Without waiting for an answer from Noce, Wagner walked down the cemetery path.

"Mmmahh!" sighed *Padre* Larusso with mock indignation at this departure, meaning: 'What should we make of this?'

"Come this way, it's right over here ..."

The *Padre* guided his companion by gently pressing on his right shoulder, directing him onto a side path that led to what was supposedly his friend's final resting place.

XIV

When she arrived at the Pertini family grave, Nobile lingered for a few minutes – and not just to keep her cover. She also remembered the *Anni di Piombo* with Pertini. A time of political and social unrest in Italy, marked by right-wing and left-wing terrorism. This period lasted until the late 1980s and reached a sad climax in 1980 when 85 people were killed in an attack on the Bologna train station.

At the same time, at the end of the 1970s, the Sicilian mafia had left a trail of blood through Palermo. To demonstrate their power, the Corleonesi killed the Palermo police chief in July 1979. Sandro Pertini had only been in office for two weeks. Two months later, the investigating judge Cesare Terranova was shot dead in his car. In January 1980, the next prominent victim was the President of the Sicilian Region, Piersanti Mattarella, who was murdered in front of his house in Palermo. He was the brother of the current President of the Republic, Sergio Mattarella.

For many young people of that era, including Nobile's father, these political and criminal assassinations of the early 1980s served as a powerful incentive to join the police or the *Carabinieri*. A generation later, Nobile had also joined the police, driven by the desire to make a difference.

She heard a branch break on the ground behind her, but wasn't concerned. Nobile had recognised from the scent who was approaching from behind. Since she and Wagner couldn't be sure whether they were being watched, they stayed in their roles.

"Excuse me, can you please tell me if it's allowed to take photos of a grave in Italy?"

"That depends."

"Let's say I want to capture something for posterity," Wagner replied, emphasising the word "capture."

"In that case, you need to make sure that you've got the right grave. Just taking a lot of photos won't work."

"I'm absolutely sure that it is the right grave and I want to capture this moment."

Nobile turned towards the church tower, where her colleague had been following the conversation via a wireless transmitter.

"I understand this as an order to proceed with the take-down. Please confirm!" he said quietly to Nobile.

"Then I wish you good luck with the photographs."

Nobile turned again towards the church tower and nodded her head.

"But don't wait too long; it looks like it might rain soon."

Nobile's colleague grabbed the radio to inform the mobile unit that they were authorised to proceed.

Wagner took a small notepad out of her bag and began writing while Nobile left the cemetery through the back entrance.

Two plainclothes police officers positioned themselves near the Fiat Panda and waited for Noce to return to his car. They wanted to take him there by surprise.

With a growing sense of unease, *Padre* Larusso had accompanied the man he knew to be a wanted criminal to the narrow path from which the empty grave could be seen. The *Padre* hoped fervently that the man wouldn't ask him to pray with him, thereby making him an accomplice in this deception.

To be on the safe side, he stopped and stretched out his left hand. He put his right hand in front of his chest and touched the chain with the wooden cross.

"It's right ahead. I'm sure you want to be alone."

With these words, the *Padre* took his leave and Noce took the few steps to the tomb alone.

Noce was puzzled by what he saw. That morning, when he heard the report on the radio, he had guessed the probability at over 50 percent that this might be a bluff to lure him to the hospital. So he didn't want to risk it and instead of driving straight to the *Ospedale* San Paolo, he decided to first check the cemetery and see whether there really was an empty grave. This would be a huge and risky undertaking, as he would have to leave his safe hiding place, but he needed to act. He had heard the report and he simply couldn't ignore the news about the stolen body after the exhumation.

Now that Noce was standing in front of the empty grave – a grave that had obviously not been dug recently but had existed for a long time – he was glad that he had made the journey here. However, he now had to accept that it was more likely than he first wanted to believe that he had taken the wrong skeleton from the hospital after all. What lay in the trunk of his Fiat Panda was now nothing more to him than a pile of old bones. *U Muto* crossed himself in front of the empty grave and made his way back to the exit.

Andrea Wagner had withdrawn as agreed and was walking towards the guesthouse where her car was parked.

Meanwhile, Nobile climbed the church tower to direct the operation from there. When she got to the top, she informed Bonfatti of the impending takedown.

"Noce is approaching the exit. About 400 metres more ... 300 metres ... He's gone through the exit and is walking towards the car."

"We'll have him soon," whispered the policeman on the bell tower.

"*Merda, tutti fermi,*" called Nobile.

"What's going on?" asked Bonfatti.

"There's a school class coming."

Wagner could now also clearly hear the cheerful singing of the group of children approaching from the top of the street.

"*Giro, giro tondo ...*" She recognised the melody as 'Ring-a-ring o' roses'.

"*Casca il mondo ...*" the children sang, now about 100 metres away from the Fiat Panda.

"*Casca la terra ...*"

"Do we know if Noce is armed?"

"Negative, *Signor Commissario*. We didn't see a weapon, but we can't rule out that has one."

Bonfatti was annoyed that he wasn't there himself. He didn't have a clear picture of the situation and had to rely on what he was hearing.

"Your operation, your decision, *Ispettore*."

Nobile looked over to Wagner, who seemed to be engrossed in conversation with the blonde woman, but who was carefully monitoring the situation on the street out of the corner of her eye.

Wagner turned towards the church tower and shook her head.

"Abort, I repeat abort. Stand down."

Nobile took a deep breath.

"Unit one: You drive ahead in the direction of Savona and let Noce overtake you if he drives in that direction. Unit two: Wait until he starts driving and stay with him. Units three and four: Wait on the Strada Provinziale at start of Albisola Superiore and take over from there. I'll follow from a distance."

"Well done, Nobile," thought Bonfatti.

Nobile and her colleague waited until Noce and the Panda were out of sight and then climbed down from the church tower. Wagner got into the patrol car with *Ispettore* Nobile while her colleague took over Wagner's car. The woman in the blue dress stood there, looking at the two cars in amazement.

*

In the patrol car in front of the post office, the first drops of rain started on the windshield and tapped softly on the hood of the car ... Tap-tap, tap-tap ...

"What do we do now?" asked Sestri.

"What police officers always do – we wait," said Caponnetto.

"It's just like the movies: three cops sitting in a car, waiting for something to happen. All that's missing are the doughnuts!" retorted Bonfatti.

"Good idea, boss! I'll go and get some, I saw a supermarket back there!"

"Sestri, close the door. I was just kidding. We'll stay here and wait!"

"Uh ... so no doughnuts?"

Caponnetto grinned. How he missed this life!

*

It would take *Ispettore* Nobile and Andrea Wagner about half an hour to get to Savona. Nobile wanted to use the time to find out more about how the police and the tasks of special investigators are organised in Germany. During her training for the senior officer career path, she had heard that there were differences between Italy and Germany in many areas, but she didn't know any details.

During their journey, Wagner gave her colleague a crash course on federalism and German police law. She explained that in Germany, targeted fugitive searches refer to intensive search operations by state criminal police offices or the Federal Criminal Police Office, and that two criteria have to be fulfilled: it must always involve persons who have already been identified, and their arrest must be of particular importance. Any police authority, public prosecutor, court or the Federal Public Prosecutor General can submit a request to include a person in a targeted search operation. Depending on the case, one of the state criminal police offices or the Federal Criminal Police Office will then respond. Special investigators take on these difficult cases and, if necessary, track the fugitives they are targeting for years and often across borders.

"And how did you get involved in this case?" asked Nobile when Wagner had finished her summary.

"This isn't a normal operation. Special investigators usually work in teams of two."

"So why are you here alone?" asked Nobile.

"There's likely to be a bigger issue behind it, something which the Bavarian State Criminal Police Office and the Italian authorities are collaborating on and which probably involves my department. I wasn't told anything about it. I just heard that a general of the *Carabinieri* is involved and has insisted that I be included. As I said, it's not a normal operation. I'm not permanently in 52."

Nobile looked at her and Wagner realised that her Italian colleague didn't know what the abbreviation meant.

"Department 52 is responsible for forensics and targeted search operations at the Bavarian State Criminal Police Office. Amongst other things, it's responsible for witness protection and tracking down wanted people. I was moved to 52... let's just say I'm on loan."

"Like a football player to another club?" asked Nobile.

"What do you mean?"

"Well, how can I explain it? Sometimes, when players need to get back into shape after a long break or they've had a disagreement with the coach, they are loaned from one football club to another – sometimes in the same league, for example the *Seria A*, the top professional football league in Italy, or to a club abroad."

"Ah, I see! Yes, something like that," replied Wagner, laughing.

"And do you like being a special investigator?"

"How can I put it? In many ways it's like normal criminal investigation work: the investigators create a personagram, a dossier of everything there is to know about the target person that can help to track them down. For example, does he or she prefer a certain make of car or a particular model? What does the person like to eat, what sports do they like, which languages do they speak? Where have they lived? Do they smoke, which brand of cigarettes do they prefer? What's their shoe and clothing size? Do they have any identifying features that are difficult to change, such as scars?"

"Whether the person is attracted to men or women," added Nobile.

"Yes, that too," confirmed Wagner.

"And what other departments do you work for?" Nobile wanted to know.

The patrol car drove along Corso Giuseppe Mazzini through Albisola Superiore, under the E80 and the railway lines, past the archaeological site of the Villa Romana di Alba Docilia.

A cat was lying in the shade of a bench in Piazza Dante Alighieri. The spring sun was shining brightly as the car turned into Corso Filippo Ferrari at the roundabout.

"Department 62: Organised crime, focus on counterfeit money."

Nobile pricked up her ears. Of course she had heard about the raids in Campagnia where counterfeit money-printing operations were repeatedly uncovered.

Most recently, in May of last year, the *Carabinieri* seized almost a million counterfeit 50-euro notes from a printing operation in Naples. In recognition of the high quality of the counterfeit notes, which also had security features such as watermarks, holograms and micro printing, the authorities had established the name 'Napoli Class' as a kind of gold standard for this type of counterfeit money.

"Fake money – is it even worth doing nowadays?"

"The question is rather, for whom is it still worth something today?" Wagner replied.

"And? For whom *is* it still worth it?"

"Well, that's the fascinating thing about this topic. For the manufacturers, counterfeit money is only worth doing in the mass market."

"What do you mean?"

"The counterfeiters get 14 to 16 euros when they sell a single fake 100-euro note. They have to put a lot into circulation to cover all the middlemen and production costs and still make enough profit – compared to the returns from other criminal activities."

"What's so fascinating about that?"

"The interesting thing is the buyers. Precisely because the manufacturers have to sell a large quantity – they don't go to the bakery around the corner to pay for their *focaccia* with the fake 100-euro note…"

"…but they sell the fakes in large quantities to other criminals. Follow the money!" Nobile had a lightbulb moment!

It was Judge Giovanni Falcone who had advocated the use of 'Follow the Money' as an investigative method in Palermo in the 1980s. After forcing banks to hand over documents on transfers and exchanges of Italian lira into US dollars, he was able to trace financial flows and uncover connections between criminal groups that had previously stayed hidden from investigators. Wagner, who had intensively studied the work of Palermo's anti-mafia pool during her training, now knew that Nobile had understood and knew something about this too.

"Where you find a lot of counterfeit money, you can assume that there are close connections to organised crime – right?" asked Nobile.

"Exactly, a criminal who, for example, wants to pay a bribe or buy something illegal and only pays 10,000 euros in real money instead of 50,000 euros saves a lot!" confirmed Wagner and continued the thought: "Even if the other party realises that a large part of the money is counterfeit, they are unlikely to go to the police."

"Well, it sounds as if you enjoy your job," remarked Nobile.

"Job? It's not just a job for me. My father always said, whatever you do in life, it's all or nothing."

Nobile giggled, "Like Master Yoda," and Wagner added in a croaking voice, "Try not. Do or do not, there is no try."

They both laughed.

"Joking aside," Wagner's voice dropped, "the service and the different roles have changed my life – especially my time in the personal protection unit, but also now in the investigation department. Whenever I check into a hotel, I pay attention to how close my room is to a stairwell and whether the window faces the courtyard or the street. You can usually specify these preferences when making the reservation but it's not so easy to get a room on the right floor, especially if you're undercover."

"Right floor?" asked Nobile uncertainly.

"You see, Francesca, hotels are 'soft targets'. They have little security and are semi-public spaces which makes them vulnerable to attack by terrorists and criminals. On the upper floors, which are too high to be able to jump out of the window, the escape options are very limited…"

"And on the ground floor you're highly exposed because attackers can break in more easily and you have less time to react," concluded Nobile.

"Exactly!"

"I think I get what you mean. Since I attended this seminar on the counterfeiting of foodstuffs in Bologna, mozzarella is no longer just a soft cheese for me."

"Ah, the *Agromafia* – it's great that you are continuing your education in this area! The topic is massively underestimated in Germany. How much longer until we arrive, Francesca?"

"We're almost in Savona. The toll booth is up ahead!"

*

Tactical units three and four followed *U Muto* from the Albisola exit along the busy Corso Giuseppe Mazzini to Corso Filippo Ferrari. When Noce turned right into Via Garibaldi, car three reacted too late and continued along Corso Ferrari towards Torrente.

The police officers from unit three made two right turns, trying to take up the pursuit at the next intersection. But *U Muto* was no longer to be seen. Unit four had more luck.

"This is unit four."

"Come in unit four."

"Target has parked the car and entered a bar."

"House number three?" asked Caponnetto, who had meanwhile taken a seat next to Bonfatti in the back seat of the car.

"Affirmative. House number three."

"I know the place. It's a bar-restaurant. They do good fish. If we're lucky, he's having lunch and we can catch him there."

On Nobile's orders, unit three drove to Via Nino Bixio, the street parallel to Via Garibaldi. They were to park there and go on foot to the bar-restaurant while unit four would wait in the car.

Two plainclothes police entered the establishment and stood at the counter. A man was sitting at a single table between the slot machine and the toilets. This was undoubtedly a table that no one would choose voluntarily, unless they were addicted to gambling or wanted to be invisible from the street.

The two men ordered *caffè* and drained the cups quickly. One walked out onto the street to wait while the other headed for the toilets. As he passed, he could clearly see the man's face. It was *U Muto*.

While the policeman flushed the toilet with his right foot, he sent a text message to Nobile. He washed his hands and left the bar without looking in Noce's direction again.

X V

Fifteen minutes later, Sestri, Caponnetto and the *Commissario* parked their car in Via Garibaldi. One of the plainclothes policemen immediately walked towards them. His nod told them that Noce was still in the restaurant. Bonfatti handed his car keys to his colleague.

"A real gourmet, the gentleman," said the policeman, "he ordered a *fritto misto*, the large mixed fried fish platter!"

"Or he's waiting for someone!"

"You mean for us? Do you think he noticed he was being followed?"

The *Commissario* looked questioningly at Caponnetto.

"We'll soon find out."

Meanwhile, Nobile had also arrived and stood next to Bonfatti.

"Two officers are stationed at the entrance, two more at the ground-floor exit of the bar."

"Toilets?" asked the *Commissario*.

Only one and it only has a small tilt window."

"*Bene, bene. Grazie Ispettore!*"

Bonfatti turned to Caponnetto.

"Shall we?"

"We? Why "we"?"

"No chance, old chap. I'm not letting you go in there alone," said the *Commissario* firmly.

"What's he going to do, Antonio? Do you think he'll attack me with a knife and fork?

"This is a police operation, and as far as I know, you're no longer on active duty. I could get into trouble just because you're here – you know that very well!"

Bonfatti pointed with his left hand to Caponnetto's right hip, where the jacket was slightly protruding because of the Beretta in the holster.

Caponnetto reached back with his right hand, pulled the holster out of his belt and handed the weapon to one of the plainclothes police officers.

"Just say you needed me to identify the target."

"Don't explain my job to me," Bonfatti growled back.

Surprised by the harsh reaction, Caponnetto took a step to the side.

"After you, *Signor Commissario*."

All morning, Caponnetto had been thinking about what it would be like to be face to face with Noce again. On the way to Via Garibaldi, he had been thinking about what he would say to him when they met. Now that the moment had come, he didn't want to let Bonfatti go first.

A few metres from the bar, Caponnetto quickened his pace. First he pretended to hold the door open for the *Commissario*, but then ran off and entered the bar before Bonfatti.

"Ah, there's my old friend! Nice to see you again after such a long time. I can't wait to hear what you have to tell me!"

This set the tone for the rest of the conversation. Caponnetto patted Noce on the shoulder with his left hand, as one does with old friends, and then used the same hand to swipe a piece of fried *calamari* from his plate.

A classic *fritto misto di pesce* is made using shrimps, squid and anchovies. The fish, which has to be dried thoroughly first, is rolled in semolina or flour and fried in oil. After a few minutes, the *fritto misto di pesce* is beautifully crispy and golden on the outside, while remaining deliciously soft on the inside. Fried thin strips of vegetables or, for a lighter option, a salad are served as a side dish. It is important never to put too much fish or too many vegetables in the hot oil at once, otherwise the temperature will drop. As soon as the vegetables and fish are golden brown, they should be taken out of the pan and placed on a paper towel to drain and absorb the excess oil. Only then can the *fritto misto* be salted, otherwise the ingredients will lose their crunch.

Caponnetto turned the chair so that the back was facing forward and sat down in front of Noce with his legs spread. This also blocked his possible escape route to the exit.

The *Commissario* had recovered from the surprise and sat down opposite Noce. He reached for the lemon on Noce's plate, sprinkled a little juice on a fried anchovy and put it in his mouth.

U Muto looked left and right. He was sure that the two men hadn't come alone, and now he recognised the silhouettes of the men who had previously been at the bar. They were now standing on the street in front of the large glass pane. And he was sure there would be more policemen at the exit.

"Please, gentlemen: help yourselves," said Noce with mock generosity.

"You don't need to invite us, we'll take what we want anyway."

Caponnetto punched Noce lightly in the side below the ribs and grabbed a piece of bread from the basket. Bonfatti took two glasses from the next table, poured water from the carafe into them and handed one to Caponnetto.

"Well, old chap, we are curious to hear what you've got to say to us."

Caponnetto gave Noce another gentle prod with his left thumb in the area between the eleventh and twelfth ribs.

Now it was Noce who reached for the lemon, sprinkled a ring of squid with juice and brought it to his mouth.

Bonfatti reached into his jacket pocket and put the photos on the table showing Noce leaving the hospital. Noce shrugged.

"Ah, you're not interested? But maybe you are interested in knowing that we found the bin bag with the bones."

Caponnetto didn't miss a slight twitch under Noce's right eyelid.

"Very strange what you find in the trunk of an old Panda!" he said in Bonfatti's direction.

"And even if some people think we police officers are stupid, slow and lazy ..." Bonfatti looked directly at Noce.

"We can take a bag like that to the forensics department in no time."

Noce twitched again

"But it'll take forever to examine a pile of bones like that and identify the victim," said Caponnetto, now feigning naivety.

There was no sign of tension between him and Bonfatti. The two friends worked perfectly together. The *Commissario* drained his glass and poured himself some more water.

"My dear Caponnetto, you're thinking like a stupid peasant."

The allusion to Noce's origins from a farming village in Calabria did not fail to have its effect.

"*Basta*," croaked U Muto, "enough of this stupid chatter!"

Caponnetto stood up, turned his chair around, sat down again and leaned back. Despite his relaxed posture, he stayed alert, ready to stop Noce if he tried to escape through the door. But Noce remained seated – seemingly defeated.

"My brother-in-law!"

"I don't understand," replied the *Commissario*.

"The dead man was my brother-in-law Stefano Malaparte, the husband of my younger sister Maria."

Caponnetto and Bonfatti looked at each other in astonishment and nodded to Noce, raising their chins briefly. Caponnetto drummed the fingers of his right hand on the table and said: "You read about the excavations in the newspaper. We already know that."

Noce was surprised.

"Go on, go on. I don't have all day," urged Bonfatti, "who killed your brother-in-law, when, where, why?"

Caponnetto's face twitched. Bonfatti had unnecessarily given away how little they actually knew about the case. Caponnetto couldn't comprehend how his friend had made such a mistake.

His mind was racing. Caponnetto was thinking about what the backstory might have been. In seconds he played through various scenarios and checked them for plausibility.

Meanwhile, *U Muto* leaned back and relaxed.

"If I make a statement and answer your questions, *Signor Commissario*, what do I get in return?"

Bonfatti realised his error and looked at Caponnetto. The latter discreetly kicked him in the ankle under the table to signal that he should keep quiet.

Caponnetto now had to take the initiative. He knocked on the table again. This time with the palm of his hand.

"It's getting late. To cut this short, I suggest we skip the part with the friendly questions."

He looked at Bonfatti challengingly and kicked him again lightly under the table; this time as a request to agree with him.

"Yes, let's skip that part," the *Commissario* agreed in a strong voice after briefly clearing his throat.

The thoughts in his head kept spinning, just like the reels of the one-armed bandit on the wall opposite. When his thoughts finally settled, his mental slot machine revealed three sentences in perfect alignment:

"Noce, we know that you killed your brother-in-law Stefano Malaparte. When you found out about the excavations, you had to act. You escaped from prison to get the bones."

Bonfatti put on a poker face and considered how likely this scenario was and how Caponnetto could have come to this conclusion.

Noce drew the corners of his mouth to one side.

"You're getting on my nerves, *Capitano*!"

Caponnetto knew he was right.

"There you go," he thought and looked at Noce unmoved.

"Stefano met a girl from Eastern Europe," Noce chuckled contemptuously. "And?"

"The bosses ignored it, they wanted to let him have his fun, but then…"

"Then something happened that the bosses couldn't ignore?!"

The stupid cow turned Stefano's head and convinced him they could start a new life together. He wanted to go to the police, wanted to enter the protection program ..."

"The bosses got wind of it and ordered you to kill your sister's husband?" Caponnetto added.

Noce nodded.

"How?" asked Bonfatti. "How did the bosses find out about it?"

Noce looked stoically past the two men. Bonfatti put his left hand on Caponnetto's forearm.

"Come on, let's go. We'll inform the *Questore* and call a press conference."

The *Commissario* had landed a powerful blow with this remark. Noce shook his head like someone who had just been slapped in the face.

"It was a friend of our friends on the island. We found out through him."

"And then?" asked Caponnetto.

"The bosses didn't want Stefano's betrayal to get out, so everything had to be kept in a very tight circle. We told my sister and everyone else that Stefano had gone into hiding."

"But in reality, you killed him and buried him in Albisola," Caponnetto stated.

"Exactly. My sister didn't know about his love affair. It would have broken her heart."

"And if he really…"

"If he had become a key witness, it could have ended badly for my sister too."

U Muto forced the words out between almost closed lips.

"OK. So, you kill your brother-in-law – but why take the risk of burying him? Why not just …," the *Commissario* paused, "make the body disappear in the usual way?"

"You mean dissolve it in acid? It's not that simple, *Signor Commissario*. You need a sturdy barrel or bathtub and quite a few litres of acid. Then it takes a while for a body to dissolve completely, and even then there some bits would be left."

"That means you would need a safe hiding place, and you didn't have one around here," Caponnetto took up the idea.

"Exactly, and besides, Stefano was my sister's husband. Even if he had made a serious mistake, I thought that as a good Christian he at least deserved a grave."

'Great double standards,' thought Caponnetto.

"And you buried him under the ruins of an ancient villa. A very fine grave indeed," he said mockingly.

"Well, I thought he'd be undisturbed for a hundred years. If I'd buried him in some field and someone had built a housing estate or shopping centre there…"

"And what did you tell your sister?"

We told her and everyone else that Stefano was in the mountains and that he was fine. I passed on messages to her from time to time."

"Messages that you wrote yourself!"

"Yes, I gave her his greetings, said that Stefano was thinking of her, that he would come for her soon… all that kind of crap."

"And what about his girlfriend from Eastern Europe, did you tell her the same story?"

Bonfatti looked Noce in the eyes. *U Muto* clicked his tongue.

"You killed her?"

"*Signor Commissario*, we're not animals." Noce chuckled again. "We're businessmen. We left her to the Albanians," Noce grinned broadly, "they took her to one of their brothels."

Bonfatti took a deep breath. Caponnetto looked first at the *Commissario*, then at Noce.

"Back to the informant, do you know him?"

Noce clicked his tongue again.

"I told you, he was a friend of our friends."

"Your friends from Sicily?" Bonfatti asked.

Noce nodded, took a toothpick from the condiment stand and peeled off the paper.

"Believe me, *Signor Commissario*, it's better for me and for you if you don't ask any more questions."

Noce put the toothpick in his mouth.

"Shall we?" asked Noce and held out both hands to Bonfatti so that he could handcuff him.

XVI

Between 8 and 8.30 pm, Antonio Bonfatti, accompanied by Cristina Donati, Giuseppe Caponnetto, Andrea Wagner and Francesca Nobile, arrived one after the other at Osteria Il Golfo.

It was a mild spring evening. The sky over Liguria was glowing in soft shades of pink. As the sun slowly disappeared and the first stars came out, Giulia Lenti was still burning with resentment and didn't even try to hide her anger.

"Well, I must say: That idiot has got a nerve! Calls here and reserves a table for five in his name!" she said to Concetta.

Antonio Bonfatti and Cristina Donati were completely in the dark about the encounter between Caponnetto and Giulia the day before. Nor did they know that Giulia had driven up to Caponnetto's place that morning with a bag of brioche – exactly at the moment when he came out of the house accompanied by a red-haired woman. The two were so engrossed in their conversation that they didn't even notice Giulia.

In Giulia's case, however, the sting was deep and went straight to her heart, where it had been niggling incessantly since the morning, steadily making the wound even worse.

With a resolute grip, she took two water glasses and a carafe from the tray, setting them down firmly on the table in front of her astonished guests. Bonfatti and Donati looked at each other uncertainly.

"Everything OK, Giulia?"

"Yes, of course, EVERYTHING is OK, what else?" The answer came half hissed, half tearful. Bonfatti was just about to ask another question when Cristina put her hand on his lap. She stood up and went after Giulia, who had hurried away from the terrace towards the kitchen.

"What an idiot," sobbed Giulia when Cristina caught up with her and put a hand on her shoulder.

"At lunchtime he tells me all sorts of things, but by nightfall, everything is forgotten and he fucks whoever is available. *Che stronzo!*"

From the corner of her eye, Cristina could see that Caponnetto had just entered the terrace, accompanied by two women.

"It's probably all just a misunderstanding that can be cleared up very easily," she tried to cheer Giulia up. "I'll talk to him, OK?"

"He can go to hell, the bastard."

'I'll take that generously as a yes,' thought Cristina and waved Concetta over. The kitchen helper had been curiously watching the scene from a few metres away and was now trotting reluctantly towards Giulia and Cristina.

Bonfatti, who had risen to greet them, was standing next to Wagner, Nobile and Caponnetto. Cristina went up to Caponnetto, put her arm around him and steered him away a few metres towards the street.

"Well, my dear Giuseppe, your love life is none of my business of course, but if we want to enjoy a meal here this evening that isn't laced with rat poison, I suggest you go and pay your respects to the lady of the house without delay."

Caponnetto looked at Cristina in surprise and shook his head slightly.

"I don't understand a thing. Giulia and I had a chat yesterday, well, we were ... Then you called and I left immediately. I haven't seen Giulia since."

"It's not me you have to explain it to. You should talk to her. Giulia thinks you're having an affair with another woman, what do I know?! She must have seen you together at your house!"

Caponnetto looked over at Andrea Wagner, who was talking to Francesca Nobile; her head tilted slightly to the side while she playfully ran her left hand through her red hair.

Concetta broke away from Giulia when she saw Caponnetto coming, went towards him and held up her hands in front of her, defensively.

"It might be better if you and your guests came another time ..."

"Giulia, please. Talk to me!"

Caponnetto pushed the assistant cook aside.

"It's true. There *was* a woman staying with me, but it's not what you think. She's a colleague. The German police made a mistake when booking a hotel for her and I offered her my guest room."

After a short pause, he added: "Giulia, please!"

Giulia turned around and rubbed her red eyes. Her smeared mascara left dark streaks on her cheeks.

"A policewoman from Germany, you say?"

"Yes, Hering sent her. Manfredo from Munich. I told you about him. We were all on an operation together today!"

"What do you mean? What kind of operation? You're retired!"

"Oh, *Amore*. Once a policeman, always a policeman."

She smiled. Caponnetto took her head between his hands and kissed her forehead. Giulia pulled him towards her and kissed him on the mouth.

Behind them, Concetta cleared her throat, first quietly, then a little louder because the couple was ignoring her.

"Hrmm ... Ahem."

Finally, she tapped Caponnetto on the shoulder.

"Now stop kissing. It's nice that everything is cleared up, but as the saying goes, *Pancia piena, cuore contento*."

Concetta's reminding them of the saying that a full stomach is the way to a happy heart hit the couple like a bucket of cold water. Caponnetto and Giulia broke their embrace.

Giulia ran her palms over her apron twice, three times to smooth it out, then went to the bathroom to wash her face and repair her makeup. Caponnetto turned to Concetta and raised his right index finger in a playful, threatening gesture.

"As for you, I hope you're going to pull out all the stops and cook something delicious!"

He gently pinched the old lady's cheek.

"But not too delicious, you know the way to a man's heart is through his stomach. I don't want to end up falling in love with you too."

Concetta grinned crookedly and waved the tea towel in her hand to chase Caponnetto out of the kitchen like an annoying fly.

Meanwhile, on the terrace, the *Commissario* had finished telling the story of how it all played out.

"... then Noce held out his hands to me."

"And what did you do?" asked Wagner.

Bonfatti laughed. "Me? Nothing at all! Caponnetto was faster: he grabbed Noce's right hand and pressed it against his chest. Noce tipped backwards and Caponnetto swept the chair leg from under him. As he fell, Noce pulled the tablecloth off. There was a terrible mess!"

Bonfatti squirmed around on his chair to recreate the scene, but without pulling the plate, carafe, bread basket and condiment holder off the table. The others laughed.

"Then Caponnetto bent down and whispered something in his ear."

"What did he say?" Nobile wanted to know.

"I don't know myself. But hopefully we'll find out as soon as he returns." The *Commissario* pointed to Caponnetto. "In any case, Noce suddenly turned very pale."

Giulia approached their table. She had Caponnetto in one hand and four menus in the other.

"Giuseppe, what did you say to Noce that frightened him so much?" asked Cristina Donati.

"I reminded him that I'm no longer on active service and am at liberty to do whatever I want."

"And that's why he turned pale?" asked Wagner, surprised.

"I told him that I could, for example, talk to the press and spread rumours that *U Muto* is now cooperating with the police, or that on my days off – of which I have plenty – I can drive to Calabria to visit his sister ..."

Bonfatti added: "And express your condolences to her. *Già*, now I understand why Noce turned pale."

"I gave him a deadline of 9 am tomorrow morning."

"And you think he'll cave in?" asked Nobile.

"*Mah*," said Caponnetto, running the back of his right hand from the base of his neck to his chin. Wagner looked over at Nobile and whispered, "I speak Italian and can make myself understood quite well, but I haven't got a clue what that means" – Wagner imitated Caponnetto's gesture somewhat furtively – "I don't get it."

"What does it look like?" asked Caponnetto, who had been watching her.

"Well, somehow it looks like you don't care, but I don't understand why."

"*Brava*, your Italian is better than you think: I don't need his cooperation, but I would be happy if he went down on his knees."

Wagner started to ask a question, but Caponnetto stopped her.

"Tomorrow is tomorrow. Now we want to eat something and celebrate that we caught Noce."

Cristina pushed the water jug aside, opened her menu and turned to Giulia.

"What do you recommend in celebration of the day?"

*

As Caponnetto and his friends rose from the table in the *osteria*, a message arrived on his mobile phone. At the same moment, Bonfatti received the same message.

The officer on duty informed them that Noce would like to speak to Caponnetto before being taken to the airport in Genoa in the morning.

Bonfatti looked at Caponnetto and raised his chin – a gesture that meant something like: "What do you think?!"

Caponnetto smiled mischievously, put his arm around Giulia's shoulder and said:

"Then I'll see you tomorrow at 9 am in the *Questura, Signor Commissario?*"

XVII

A jug can hold water, wine or milk. Its shape stays the same, regardless of its purpose. The jug does not change its shape; it cannot change it and has no influence on what its shape holds. People, on the other hand, can change shape – and also what's inside them. They can develop and decide for themselves what constitutes their shape and contents. They can be good, improve, or give up. And even if a person doesn't change, they are still the ones to make that decision.

While Caponnetto was musing on these and other thoughts, he looked for the Moka in Giulia's kitchen, filled it and put it on the stove. Giulia was still asleep and he wanted it to stay that way. When she woke up later, he would already be at the Savona police headquarters.

*

Caponnetto was looking around the *Questura's* interview room as if he was waiting for the person opposite him to ask him what he was looking for.

And just as *U* Muto was about to ask the question, Caponnetto beat him to the answer.

"It's a shame that smoking is no longer allowed here," he said, waiting a moment longer than usual.

"I didn't know you smoked, *Capitano*," the man said between half-closed lips.

"I don't, but then the scene here would be much more dramatic. Then I would have lit this piece of paper here," Caponnetto held the folded piece of paper out to Noce, "the piece of paper with the message you wrote me, like your friends do with the Madonna pictures." Caponnetto was referring to an initiation ritual that was common in both the Sicilian *Cosa Nostra* and the Calabrian *'Ndrangheta*.

"That's how it's done, Noce, isn't it? The recruit pledges secrecy and loyalty to the family. An image of a saint is used, particularly that of the Virgin Mary. The image is kissed and sometimes a little blood is sprinkled over it from a cut in the finger."

"You watch too many crime thrillers," said Noce.

"And then the picture is burned and the recruit has to hold it in his hands – just as he should burn like the picture if he breaks his oath of loyalty."

As Caponnetto said this, he tore up the piece of paper that Noce had given him at the beginning of the meeting into many small pieces and placed them on the table in front of him like a puzzle. Noce, completely taken aback, pushed the pieces of paper away from him as if they were crawling insects that disgusted him. Caponnetto looked at the clock on the wall.

"Well, it's getting late. We both have a long journey ahead of us. You back to Germany and I – well, you know how long that journey takes: It's quite a long way to San Luca!"

Noce looked at him dumbfounded.

"Judging by her voice, your sister is much younger than you. I'm very curious to see what she looks like."

"You swine, we had an agreement! I kept my part of the bargain."

"You wrote a number or a name on a piece of paper that I never read," he pointed to the scraps.

"So why shouldn't I tell poor Maria what she has long suspected: that her dear Stefano is dead."

"You won't tell her that I killed her husband," raged Noce.

Caponnetto continued in a firm, loud voice, "... and also hand over Stefano's bones to Maria. Then she can bury her husband and visit his grave every day if she chooses."

Overwhelmed by anger and rage, Noce croaked, "There was an important number on that piece of paper. You're going to regret that, *Capitano*. *Ti apro come una cozza!*"

The guard standing at the door was amused. He hadn't heard that vulgar expression for a long time. To 'open someone like a clam' was to threaten to tear them to pieces because clams are difficult to open if you don't have the right technique. He thought of how he and the neighbourhood kids had shouted the phrase to each other while playing in the street when they couldn't agree on something and one of them wanted to look very strong.

Caponnetto, who knew the saying from more than just his childhood, remained undaunted.

"Really, Noce, I would have expected you to know me better than that."

Caponnetto stood up. The guard immediately prepared to open the door.

"Murder is a criminal offence, and you confessed to the murder of your brother-in-law. I'm not a man of honour, at least not as you understand the word. I am

Giuseppe Caponnetto," he added quietly, "ex-*Capitano* of the *Carabinieri*."

Caponnetto turned his back on Noce and went to the door.

"I don't even need to call the number on the piece of paper. I can imagine whose voice I would hear."

"How long have you known?" hissed *U Muto*, irritated.

Caponnetto paused briefly at the threshold and raised his right hand. Without turning around, he whispered: "*A Dio* Noce, *A Dio*."

*

EPILOGUE

Wagner's phone rang. She looked at the display and was surprised.

"Excuse me, it's my boss," she said, standing up.

"Give him my regards!" Caponnetto smiled.

"It's not Hering. It's my boss in the 62."

She took the call and walked a few metres towards the street. Nobile, Bonfatti, and Caponnetto, who were meeting Wagner for a farewell lunch in the Osteria Il Golfo, could only hear the investigator saying "Hello" from a distance.

Nobile looked into two questioning faces and said, trying to sound as casual as possible, "I think she means the department at the Bavarian State Criminal Police: Department 62 is the department for organised crime specialising in counterfeit money."

A few metres away, Andrea Wagner was listening to the sonorous, good-natured voice of her boss.

"Good work, Wagner. Do you remember what I told you on your first day with us?"

"That you sometimes act like an ass, but you don't mean it?"

"No, I never said that!" he replied with mock indignation.

"Oh, so you mean the other thing: that you would never lie to me, but maybe you wouldn't always tell me the whole truth straight away?"

"Yes, now we're on the same page."

'Strange guy,' thought Wagner, and was curious to see what unknown truth her boss would reveal next.

"It's like this, Wagner: A few weeks ago, an attentive employee at a bank in Munich informed us that various people had deposited cash there in several tranches, always just below the limit of the amount that would need to be reported."

"So why did he report it? Did all the deposits go to the same account?"

"No, they went to different accounts, but the employee became suspicious of one of the first deposits because it was only in 50-euro notes. He then secretly marked one note."

"And he took it to the police," added Wagner. "Let me guess: it was counterfeit!"

"Yes, but not just any counterfeit. The bank employee could see that it was of the highest quality!"

"Napoli class?" asked Wagner, electrified.

"Bingo!"

"And then you checked the other deposits and found even more fake money."

"Yes, exactly, and we looked at the money flows during the past 18 months and came across an ongoing investigation by our Italian colleagues."

'Follow the money,' thought Wagner.

"So let me guess: all the deposits ended up with two or three recipients."

"Two to be exact, one was a middleman who in turn passed the money on to arms dealers."

"And the other recipient?"

"His trail ends in Genoa. It's complicated, but we and our Italian colleagues from the anti-mafia agency *DIA* and the *Carabinieri ROS* suspect that the money was used to bribe an official, possibly someone in the judiciary system."

Wagner's pulse quickened. Then her boss finally asked the question she had been hoping for.

"Would you mind if we extended your deployment in Liguria? I'm thinking weeks rather than days."

"And Hering?" Wagner asked hesitantly.

"*Kriminalhauptkommissar* Hering has been informed. He congratulates you on the capture of Simone Noce and fully supports this investigation and your deployment."

Wagner looked over at the *osteria* and the convivial group at the table. Her red hair fluttered in the wind.

"And who will I be working with here locally?"

"That's still being sorted out. You know how complicated it is with the authorities in Italy: *Polizia di Stato*, *Carabinieri*, financial police. The anti-mafia agency DIA is in charge and is supposed to be coordinating the police agencies, but it's…"

"… complicated. Yes, you already said." Her boss's tendency to repeat himself made her nervous, she sensed her impatience.

"Well, if you think I'm still needed here, of course I'll do it. Detailed briefing on Monday?" Wagner tried to end the conversation on a friendly note.

"10 am. Not a word to anyone until then," said the head of 62 firmly and ended the conversation. He raised his right thumb. *Kriminalhauptkommissar* Hering, who was sitting opposite him, gave a satisfied smile.

As Wagner approached the table again, Caponnetto came towards her. He had been to the gents and now, instead of going straight to the others at the table, he made a detour and walked towards Wagner.

"*Tutto bene*?" he asked.

"Yes, everything's fine." She smiled. "I just can't talk about it, at least not yet. But yes, *tutto bene*!"

"I'm glad to hear it, Rea. You are a good police officer and a good person. You deserve to be fine!" said Caponnetto.

Wagner was surprised by this unexpected compliment and the empathy that Caponnetto showed.

At first she couldn't think of anything better than to salute, bringing her right hand to her temple and then quickly pushing it forward.

"I hope you're fine too," she said and added, "you know, *Capitano*, my grandfather often used to say something to me that I didn't quite understand when I was younger."

She looked over at the table.

"But now you do? I'm all ears!" replied Caponnetto.

"My grandfather said: You only come across a few good trains in life. These few good trains can go in very different directions, but they all have one thing in common: you have to go to the station to get on board."

Caponnetto silently squeezed Wagner's hand and walked towards the street. As he walked away, he called out, "Please send my apologies to the others. There's something important I need to do."

*

In the back seat of the black SUV, Marini's fingers flew rhythmically over the centre console. The general drummed the rhythm of the Radetzky March: tatatum, tatatum, tatatum-tum-tum ...

He opened the window with his left hand and at once felt the sea breeze on his cheeks, smelled the sweet scent, tasted the salty air.

When he heard the ping of an incoming message, he stopped drumming and reached for the mobile phone that his driver wordlessly handed back to him.

Generale Marini read the message and nodded in satisfaction.

"Welcome home, Giuseppe," he said quietly. "Welcome home."

A gentle tap with two fingers next to the driver's neck rest sufficed. The convoy set off towards Savona.